TESTAMENT

Jose Nateras

A NineStar Press Publication

Published by NineStar Press
P.O. Box 91792,
Albuquerque, New Mexico, 87199 USA.
www.ninestarpress.com

Testament

Printed in the USA
First Edition
December, 2019

Print ISBN: 978-1-951880-15-6

Also available in eBook, ISBN: 978-1-951880-10-1

Warning: This book contains sexual content, which may only be suitable for mature readers, and depictions of workplace harassment, a suicide attempt, sexual assault, and assault.

Gabe Espinosa, is trying to dig himself out of the darkness. Struggling with the emotional fallout of a breakup with his ex-boyfriend, Gabe returns to his job at The Rosebriar Room; the fine dining restaurant at the historic Sentinel Club Chicago Hotel. Already haunted by the ghosts of his severed relationship, he's drastically unprepared for the ghosts of The Sentinel Club to focus their attentions on him as well.

When a hotel guest violently attacks Gabe, he finds himself the target of a dark entity's rage; a rage built upon ages of racial tension and toxic masculinity. Desperate to escape the dark spiral he's found himself in, Gabe flees across the city of Chicago and dives into the history of the hotel itself. Now, Gabe must push himself to confront the sort of evil that transcends relationships and time, the sort of evil that causes damage that ripples across lives for generations.

Gabe must fight to break free from the dark legacy of the past; both his own and that of the hotel he works in.

This novel is dedicated to the City of Chicago, as well as my family: Mom, Dad, Raquel, and the whole gang. I also have to thank my friends (Bryce, Zeke, Michael, Brian, Sara, and Elena). Much thanks to Cina Pelayo for supporting a fellow Latinx horror writer—your insight has been invaluable.

Chapter One

I pulled out my phone and checked the time. I needed to be at work at six thirty, and unless the train started moving within the next five seconds, I would be late. A commute that usually took thirty minutes, door to door, was stretching closer and closer to taking forty minutes. Still, the train sat there, idle in its dark underground tunnel. There's nothing worse than being late and getting stuck on a delayed train car at six fifteen in the morning. Fuck.

I rocked back and forth impatiently, a loose rivet in my seat clicking arrhythmically in its socket. Most of the Chicago Transit Authority's train cars were in some state of disrepair. This car in particular had maps of the train lines missing overhead, cracked lighting fixtures, fractured chrome, and unsecured hardware. The homeless man stretched out asleep across the seats at the other end of the car didn't seem to care. Neither did the middle-aged nurse sitting kitty-corner from me, listening to music on her phone through bright-pink earbuds.

I took a deep breath to stop my agitated rocking. The thick smell of synthetic flowers wafted along the length of the train car. An otherwise pleasant smell, in the enclosed space of the train car the scent was overwhelming, almost sickening. It had to be coming from the nurse. How'd I not notice the strength of her perfume sooner?

It occurred to me, if I puked on the 'L' right then and there, I'd have no excuse but to call in sick. It wouldn't be the first time someone threw up on the Blue Line. I wouldn't even have to *actually* vomit. I could just call in, hop off the train at the next stop, and grab the next one headed back toward my apartment. Tempting, but I could practically hear the voice of my manager Leslie. "Really, Gabe? What the fuck? Aren't you *just* coming back from an extended leave of absence, *Mr. Espinosa*?"

With the sound of metal grinding on metal, the train started to move. I closed my eyes, allowing the momentum to build and hurdle me toward the misery of employment in the service industry.

Maybe misery was an exaggeration. As the train came to an abrupt stop at the Monroe station, I tried to remind myself there were worse fields to work in. Six blocks stretched between the train platform and the Sentinel Club Hotel. More specifically, six blocks stretched between me and the hotel's restaurant, the Rosebriar Room, where I worked as a host. Walking so far would typically take around nine minutes, and at 6:25 a.m., I only had five minutes to do so. Officially late, I somehow found the energy to hustle up the stairs from the underground train platform and race out into the November chill.

I found myself caught behind a herd of Chicago commuters: business-bros and cubicle drones trotting to their respective jobs scattered across the Loop. Dodging between the office workers drowsily heading to work, I sprinted through the concrete canyon of downtown skyscrapers.

It was still dark. Only after I made it to Michigan Avenue, across from the green expanse of Millennium

Park, could I see the first streaks of orange in the dark-gray sky. I pulled out my phone again. 6:31 a.m. "Shit."

Speeding through the front doors of the hotel, I hurried to the service elevator. With no time to stop at the staff locker room down in the basement, I headed straight up to the thirteenth floor.

People often say hotels are naturally creepy places. I hadn't really thought about it one way or another until I started working in one. It was true. The Sentinel Club Chicago was creepy, and being one of the oldest buildings in the city only made it all the more eerie. Before becoming a boutique hotel, the SCC was a historied private men's club, and the Rosebriar Room, now the hotel's wood-paneled fine-dining restaurant, once served as the private dining room for the club's most elite members.

I'd been working there for a year and a half or so, and things I hadn't noticed at first had started to weigh on my mind. More and more I found myself aware of the creepiness of the place. A laugh echoing in quiet, empty rooms. A flicker of movement out of the corner of an eye. A shadow on a wall with no one there to cast it. The feeling of being watched.

The prospect of spending my morning in such a place sounded pretty miserable. Perhaps I hadn't been so far off in describing my job as a "misery" after all.

With a *ding*, the elevator doors parted, and I stepped into the restaurant's vestibule. Spherical lighting fixtures hung from the ceiling, velvet-wallpaper lined the walls, and a couple of plush leather armchairs formed a small waiting area just outside a set of frosted glass double doors. The burgundy, paisley pattern embossed on the wallpaper caught the light with a silky sheen, making the walls look wet.

Leslie loved to open the doors as soon as she arrived, regardless of whether or not breakfast service had actually begun. Since the doors were closed, I could safely assume she hadn't gotten there yet: a comforting thought. Dealing with my manager ranked among my least favorite things. Right up there with escorting clueless patrons to the bathroom and maintaining a cordial smile while being berated by an unhappy privileged guest dissatisfied with the table they'd reserved for themselves. I pushed through the doors and made my way into the restaurant.

Something about the place's overlapping layers of history made me uneasy. Not just in the Rosebriar Room, but throughout the hotel. As I walked through the empty restaurant toward the point-of-sale to clock in, I couldn't help but imagine the place as it had been years ago when it still served as the club's private dining room. I could easily picture empty chairs and tables occupied by rich white men in waistcoats and top hats, eating caviar and drinking martinis thirteen floors above the rushing bodies and vehicles of Michigan Avenue.

A prime location. Built as a part of the development surrounding the World's Fair in 1893, the building was a testament to Chicago architecture. Where else should it be, but right on Michigan Avenue? And where else would a group of Chicago's most affluent and influential gentlemen want to have their clubhouse?

Thinking about the sort of things elite, moneyed people do in private is a dangerous road to go down. The hospitality group's efforts to recreate and modernize the original club's decor only made picturing the sordid details of the past all too easy. I didn't like to imagine the nefarious deeds rich white men indulged in while tucked away in the shadowy, mahogany-walled corners of the

Sentinel Club's numerous private lounges and parlors. I'd seen *Eyes Wide Shut*. Though no longer a private club, the hotel still attracted a predominantly privileged, demanding clientele. Dealing with their bullshit was hard enough without images of sinister, masked orgies running around in my head.

After the club ceased operating in 2009, the hotel group responsible for the restoration and updating of the building did its damnedest to maintain as much of the original aesthetic as they could. They spun the club's old-school style into achingly modern, hipster-chic; an aesthetic torn half from an Urban Outfitters catalogue and half from a history book. In doing so, the hotel had transformed into some sort of hybrid animal. A taxidermy calf juxtaposed with some framed, ironic, postmodern screen print. A place where old and new met. Public and private. All dark wood and shining brass. Full of potential and full of the past. In such a place, one could easily forget where you were. *When* you were. From the solitude of the Rosebriar tucked away on the thirteenth floor, beyond the restored ballrooms and reconstructed athletic facilities, it was too easy to imagine the streets below being lit by gaslight with H.H. Holmes prowling the darkened alleys.

I clocked in at six forty on the dot. Ten minutes late. A healthy display of tardiness. But as long as Leslie wasn't there yet, it didn't matter all too much. I stowed my jacket and scarf away in the guest coat closet, then made sure to adjust the sleeves of my suit coat. Upon getting hired, I was required to purchase the standard H&M suit the entire front-of-house staff had to wear. Had I been excited to spend a third of my first paycheck on the outfit? No. However, cheap, yet vaguely stylish, our uniforms helped us blend into the fanciness of the establishment without drawing too much attention. Besides, a black suit was useful for all sorts of occasions: weddings, baptisms. Funerals.

I rummaged through the host stand's drawer. Digging past the notepads and boxes of business cards with the restaurant's hours of operation, I finally found the lint roller I so desperately needed and proceeded to peel the particles off my suit. "Fucking lint," I grumbled. In the stillness of the restaurant, even a mumble seemed to echo. "Shit." The tape like surface of the roller snagged on the hooked end of my bracelet.

In an effort to keep things "hip," we were free to add slight testaments to our individual personalities. Only if they weren't considered distracting and had been approved by management, of course. Cufflinks, modest jewelry, tie-bars, and the like. I looked down at my wrist where a simple leather cord was fastened. The clasp, a small steel charm in the shape of an anchor, was threaded through a loop, holding it in place.

I had worn this bracelet every day since Kenny gave it to me as an anniversary present even though we'd technically been together over a year at the time. Since then, it had practically become a part of my arm. This morning, I couldn't avoid the thought of it being two years exactly since I first received it. I tucked the bracelet into my sleeve, ensuring it didn't snag on the cotton bandage wrapped around my wrist, and tugged down my shirt sleeve. After I shoved the lint roller back in the drawer, I made my way toward the terrace windows.

Before breakfast service began, I was there alone. The dining room seemed far removed from the distant bustle of the limited, morning back-of-house staff who were confined to the isolation of the kitchen. Attempting to shake off my foul mood, I focused my attention on the sun continuing to climb over the lip of Lake Michigan's eastern horizon. Warm light spilled across Millennium Park. The light split into rays and danced through the stained Tiffany glass of the dining room's east-facing windows. The designer glass dated back to the building's construction and separated the main dining room from the terrace seating. The terrace floated there, looking down from the thirteenth floor over Michigan Avenue and the lake beyond.

After managing to pry my eyes from the view, I looked over the guest book at the day's reservations to prepare the VIP list for Chef and make the seating plan for the morning rush. I spread out the day's newspapers—*The Chicago Tribune, The Sun-Times, The Wall Street Journal*—along the bar and went on to straighten place settings.

If the settings weren't just right, Leslie would give me hell. So, I carefully adjusted each silver knife to be completely parallel with the fork beside it. Every crystal water glass had to be placed at a precise angle in relation to the rectangular fold of the linen napkin. The monogrammed plate had to be perfectly centered in the place setting. Considering how, without fail, every guest promptly dismembered the carefully arranged place settings the second they sat down, I hated the task.

With a yawn, I tried to gear up for yet another long day. Then I noticed the chill. A draft of cold air in the otherwise climate-controlled room. My muscles tensed, and a faint tickle slithered along the back of my neck and arms as my body readied itself to run. But run from what? There was nothing there. Still, I could sense something. Even though I knew the restaurant was empty, it didn't feel like it. It never felt empty.

I took a breath and willed myself to turn back toward the host stand. Just beyond my usual workstation, a heavy, ornate brass vase stood on a pedestal. To distract myself, I moved to freshen the water of the flowers it held. The vase had apparently been a fixture in the club since its founding back at the turn of the century. The thick metal of it was engraved to portray a satyr—in all its Greco-Roman, phallically exuberant glory—pouring wine from a decanter.

I hated the ugly thing. I hated the way the satyr's twisted goat horns were forged into the vase's handles. I hated the sneer on his face and the stupid joke of his giant, menacing boner. The whole thing was absurd and grotesque.

With a sigh, I pulled it down from its perch and lugged the monstrosity into the kitchen. I could change out the water in the sink at the barista station, tucked away in a dimly lit corner at the far end of the otherwise bright kitchen. There, I pulled out the nest of sunflowers and orange roses, pouring the putrid water out from the vase. The scent of rotting flowers, the reek of a funeral parlor, hit me full in the face. I turned on the faucet and used fresh water to rinse the rank fluid from the vase. I filled the brass monstrosity with cool water and tucked the flowers back into their place.

Beyond the kitchen door, I could feel the expanse of the restaurant and, for just a second, could almost hear the subtle murmur of polite dinner conversation. As calmly as my nerves would allow, I turned off the water. Peeking through the door's porthole, I tentatively looked out into the silent emptiness of the dining room.

Could a place like SCC ever really be empty? At all hours of the day and night, there are the hotel staff and guests: sleeping, awake. Somebody is always somewhere, doing something. But even if all the rooms and halls in the entire building were unoccupied and every employee called in sick, a place as old as this would always be loaded with a residue. Some kind of echo lingers. The silence is heavier. The shadows are deeper. When it's crowded and bustling and there's a ton of busy work to do, it might go unnoticed. Things are harder to ignore when you're alone.

My mind flitted back to waking up that morning and the darkness of my empty room without Kenny lying there beside me. Alone in the restaurant, I could still feel the leaden weight of my limbs as I lay in my empty bed; my mind still swimming up from the deep, shadowy waters of sleep while I tried to shake off the lingering dread of unremembered nightmares.

Even though I stood in the isolated barista station, I had the sensation of lying at home; the familiar masses of my bedroom furniture solidifying in the shadows around me. The impossible challenge of dragging myself to the edge of the bed and finding the will to get up. In the darkness, I had fumbled my phone awake, and the brightness of the screen was almost painful. Fuck mornings. Fuck waking up. Fuck my empty bed. Kenny hadn't been there since we'd broken up a month ago, but his absence was a presence in itself. Fuck that. A thought floated into my mind, simple, and inflectionless. *I wish I were dead.*

Chapter Two

Something moved behind me. The heavy cherry-wood door leading into the kitchen opened gradually, letting out a low creak, a sound I'd heard a million times before. But this time the noise hit my ear strangely, sounding familiar in a new way. An echo from time spent at my grandparents' house. Their bedroom, one of the last times I'd been there. In that moment, the door's creak reminded me of my grandfather groaning in his sleep, of the sound he would make not long before he died. I turned to face it, unable to do anything else. From around the door emerged Ernesto, the back waiter for the brunch shift. Spotting me, his cheery face broke into a grin, and I couldn't help but laugh at myself.

"You scared me!"

"*Lo siento hermano!*"

Behind him, Ernesto was lugging two empty, bronze-plated trash bins. Even the Rosebriar's garbage was fancy. As he grabbed plastic trash bags from under the sink, I found myself breathing easier.

Ernesto had the sort of jovial nature that was contagious and desperately appreciated in a place like the Sentinel Club with its perpetually heavy atmosphere. I liked him. He never gave me a hard time for my shitty Spanish. Being Mexican American, people often assumed I was bilingual. Or that I don't speak English. But Ernesto never made me feel guilty about my lack of fluency. I'd stumble through our Spanish-language interactions, and he'd listen patiently. I found the pace of his Guatemalan Spanish easier to follow than the speed and dialect of Spanish speakers from Mexico. Even when speaking with my Mexican family members in Spanish, I struggled to keep up, but Ernesto's pace was more manageable.

At five foot eight, I'm not a particularly tall guy. Yet, next to Ernesto, I might as well have been a giant. In the right pair of shoes, he stood maybe five feet tall. Maybe. His positivity and sense of humor had a way of lightening up the air, even when dragging around heavy, awkward trash cans almost the same size as him.

"You okay, Gabe? You look pale."

"I'm fine," I said, taking the heavy flower arrangement back to its spot behind the host stand. "You surprised me, that's all."

"Sorry. *Dios*, everyone here's so jumpy all the time."

"Maybe."

"No, no maybe. Did you hear about Cecilia?" Ernesto had to be at least ten years older than me. But still, his face lit up with a youthful enthusiasm as he geared up to gossip. "She got fired! She refused to go get more onions from dry storage, so they canned her, *tonta*." He shook his head with a laugh.

"Why wouldn't she go?"

"Would you go down to the basement *solo, Señor* Jumpy?" Ernesto raised a critical eyebrow. His thick Guatemalan accent gave the question a musicality, but behind the humorous glint in his eyes, something else gave me pause: a slight edge of fear.

"I go down to the locker room all the time."

"*Pues,* the locker room and cold storage are different, *hermano*." He was right. The staff locker room was also down in the basement, yes. It was at the end of a labyrinth made up entirely of white fluorescent lights, slick linoleum, and sanitized tile. Metal lined the halls, and the constant rumble of the industrial-sized laundry machines, which washed the hotel's linens, filled the air with unending vibrations.

Cold storage, on the other hand, was located on the complete other side of the underground complex's twisting halls and blind corners. Accessible by a secondary service elevator, which led straight to the kitchen of the Rosebriar, its walls were aged brick. The floor was cement, smoothed by decades' worth of footsteps that had worn down the hard finish of the paved floor. The ceilings were low, and orange sodium lamps jutted from the walls, spilling thick amber light over the cellar stocked with rations and various weird smells. The hotel was built up, layer by layer, from old to new over the years. The cellar was the oldest layer, the lowest level, and when you went down there, you could feel it.

I had been down there only one time, sent on a special mission from Chef to grab more truffles. We needed them for the baked eggs featured in some breakfast special or other. I could still remember stepping out of the elevator and feeling the sudden drop in temperature. They called it *cold* storage for a reason. The natural chill of the space is the whole point of storing food in a cellar.

Finding my way to the massive vault of the refrigerator, my mind went to a short story by Edgar Allan Poe I'd read once as a kid, "The Cask of Amontillado." I tried not to imagine being walled up alive behind the ancient brick walls, which made up the foundations of the hotel. I tried not to imagine rotting corpses and bleached bones tucked away behind the crumbling stones, which were at the roots of the Rosebriar. I tried to find those fucking truffles as fast as I could and made sure to get my ass back into the elevator as soon as possible.

"I guess you're right," I said.

Whatever fear had been in Ernesto's eyes evaporated, replaced with the familiar wariness of a man too tired to let a spooky basement keep him from doing his work.

"Damn straight. But, then again, Cecilia is a bit *loca*, you know?"

"Is she?"

"*Pues*, she got herself fired over *pinche* ghost stories. Whining about *fantasmas*. Saying '*hay mal aquí .*' It's like, no shit. There's evil everywhere. *Así es la vida.*"

Ernesto never spoke much about why he left Guatemala, but I knew about plenty of stories detailing the hard journey so many of my coworkers undertook to get to Chicago. I couldn't help but wonder about the sorts of evil he'd seen in his life. What sorts had I seen in mine? He wasn't wrong. Bad things—*evil things*—happened all the time. It's a part of life. And those bad, evil things left a mark on people. Physical and otherwise. It's not insane to think they left a mark on places too.

"*Te creas en fantasmas?*" I asked.

"*Pueeees*," he started, stretching the word out. "*Tú sabes.* Whether or not I do, I sure as fuck don't let it keep me from *trabajando. Porque trabajo es dinero, y todo el mundo se necessita dinero para vivir. Así es la vida.*"

I sensed the conversation had reached its end and followed Ernesto back into the dining room. He returned the trash cans to their designated spots in silence. In my entire time at the Rosebriar, I had never had a conversation like that with Ernesto. He hadn't cracked any jokes or made any puns. His signature laugh, loud and trumpet-like, had not once reverberated through the empty dining room as it so often did.

Done with his task, he sent a nod in my direction, then headed back into the kitchen. Cecilia had said *"There's evil here."* As the door to the kitchen swung shut behind Ernesto, leaving me alone once more, I wondered if she was right.

I returned the vase to its spot, wishing Ernesto had stuck around to shoot the shit for a bit longer. Morning back waiters always had a million things to do before service started. I doubted I'd see him again before the first rush of the day.

I took a moment to look around the dining room. Everything was so orderly and bright. Polished wood shone so cleanly you could practically see your reflection in the glossy surface of the tables and the bar that stretched along the length of the restaurant. Nouveau-rustic, brass lighting fixtures illuminated the bright room with the warm glow of Edison bulbs.

The rising sun shone through the Tiffany windows leading out to the patio. A beautiful view. A beautiful space. But I couldn't help but feel like something ugly hid behind all the polish and gloss. The room, empty and quiet except for my own breathing, was so still. It reminded me of the surface of some deep, ancient pond. Who could tell what sort of things might swim beneath the surface? Things that had been there just as long as the pond itself. Things with teeth.

I pulled out my phone to check the time. 6:45 a.m. Leslie still hadn't shown up, and the sound system was controlled from the manager's office, which was located past the kitchen in the back. Without her, I couldn't turn on the restaurant's playlist. The ultra-hip mix of songs, curated by the general manager, consisted of deep cuts from the '50s and '60s as well as contemporary indie hits. Without it playing over the top-of-the-line sound system, the restaurant sat, stuck in a palpable silence, thick and heavy. The absence of noise had formed a vacuum, which threatened to suck the air from my lungs.

Without thinking, I broke for the door. I crossed through the foyer, surprised by the urgency with which I poked the call button on the main elevator. Carefully, I forced my chest to stop heaving. It took all my attention to breathe calmly. It was completely irrational. I had no reason to be hyperventilating. I knew that. I also knew, just as acutely, that I *needed* to get out of there. If only I could get into that elevator, I'd be fine. The seconds ticked by, and I kept my eyes locked on the brass lighting fixture in the upper-right corner of the elevator's frame. I forced myself to breathe at a deliberate pace, in and out, counting each breath as I did. "One, two, three..." Finally, with a ding, the small bulb blinked alight, and the doors started to open.

I had no way to sanely articulate why I had the urgent need to keep my eyes focused directly in front of me; to resist the urge to look back. I had no logical reason for my behavior. No matter what, I would keep my gaze straight ahead. I needed to. My eyes went directly from the light indicating the elevator's arrival, to the doors opening, and then forward to the back of the elevator itself.

I acted on pure instinct, an instinct that refused to allow me to turn and face the empty restaurant behind me. Yet, some shadowy corner of my brain whispered, *Turn around and look. Look. If there's nothing there, it won't hurt to look. Idiot. What are you afraid of?* And a voice from my gut responded, *Don't do it. If you do, you might not like what you see.*

I recognized the voice. The same one used to speak to me as a child, urging me to run up the basement stairs before the shadows could drag me down into the darkness. The same voice identified the shadowy bulk in the corner of my childhood bedroom as some fanged, grinning beast rather than a pile of dirty clothes. The same voice loved to remind my lapsed-Catholic lizard brain if demons existed in the Bible, and the Bible was real, then those demons were real too.

I didn't turn around.

Instead, I walked straight onto the elevator and, without looking, stretched my left hand out. With a fumbling backward swat, I pressed the Close Door button on the panel. Forcing myself to inhale, exhale, inhale, exhale, I waited for the sound of the doors shutting before I turned around and jabbed the button for the lobby.

I was being an idiot. Heat flooded my ears and the back of my neck as the elevator ticked down floor after floor. Embarrassed but so glad to be out of the suffocating silence of the thirteenth floor, I leaned against the railing. After a moment, the elevator settled on the first level with another ding. The doors slid open, and I straightened my lapels before stepping into the lobby.

It was still early, so there weren't many people in the wide, airy hotel foyer. The floor was polished tile with fine wooden pillars and fixtures, making the whole place look like a library suited for Oxford. All along the walls, shelves and cabinets had been beautifully restored. Originals had been maintained perfectly from when the hotel—still a private club at the time—was first built. The dark oak shelves were crammed with old taxidermy, miniatures, books, globes, spy glasses, athletic statues, and framed pictures of former club members in their youth.

Tucked in the far corner, a mighty fireplace roared, surrounded by lush leather couches. Across from the bank of elevators, the main reception desk waited for an influx of hotel guests to check in, check out, request more towels, or demand directions to the Bean. Beyond reception, a sprawling, white-marble staircase led up to the mezzanine, flanked by twin marble statues of Adonis.

I approached the desk where the concierge looked down at his computer, his face reflecting the subtle blue glow of the screen. Stanley had to be the youngest of the concierge staff, maybe a year or two younger than me, but he started working here almost six months before I did. A record. I couldn't think of anyone else who had worked at SCC as long.

"Hey, Stan!"

He looked up, startled, but broke into a smile when he realized it was me and not one of the hotel's typical, high-maintenance guests. "Hey, man. For a second there I thought you were Tony."

"Your manager MIA this morning too?"

"Nah, he's here. He just ran to the Starbucks around the corner to grab his basic-ass a cappa-whatever. Leslie not in yet?"

"Nope," I said, "It's surprising too, given the fact she normally runs on WPT." We shared a laugh.

Over the years, both of us had endured countless white service industry managers making reference to "Colored People Time." It was a relief to have someone to commiserate with. Having positions like ours took its toll. Stan was Black and the concierge. Even though our experiences working here weren't entirely the same, the two of us found ourselves with a peculiar type of authority. With the sort of guests who'd readily assume any person of color in a place like the SCC must be a janitor, that authority had a weight both of us had to bear. Stan's authority over rooms and check-ins and mine over tables and reservations garnered us a sliver of respect folks like Ernesto went without. People, white people in particular, often *had* to ask us for things. Request things from us. Our positions gave us a modicum of control.

However, given the nature of the hospitality industry and of our particular jobs, we found ourselves constantly stuck accommodating with forced smiles, soothing vocal tones, and internalized existential agony. Often enough, we still ended up obligated to acquiesce our meager control to the demands of entitled guests.

He laughed. "'White People Time' ain't magic, man, and it sure as hell ain't a hangover cure. You must not have seen Leslie last night. We all hit up Rudy's for the Sunday special, and your girl had more than a few Cosmos. I'd be shocked if she *was* on time."

"Damn. A clo-pen is one thing, but to go for post-shift drinks too? What a beast."

"Yeah, dude. Who parties when they got back-to-back closing and opening shifts?" Something drew Stan's eye toward the door, and he trailed off. I turned to follow his gaze, expecting an incoming guest or even Tony, but there was no one there. Distractedly, he started, "Sorry, I thought..."

"Thought what?"

"Nothing. Was there anything you needed?"

"Needed? No. I guess not. Just to get out of the Rosebriar for a second, maybe," I said with a half-hearted laugh.

"I don't know how you do it, man."

"Do what? I deal with the same bougie white people
you do."

"I mean work up there alone. Not me."

"It is creepy," I said carefully, "but so is this whole
place. It's creepy down here too."

"Yeah, but I'm never alone down here."

I looked around. He was right. As empty as the lobby
was at its deadest, there was pretty much always someone
there. A guest. The shoeshine guy. Bellhops, parking
valets, housekeeping, security. Up in the Rosebriar, if no
guests had made it in, as was often the case on an
uneventful morning, Leslie would be in the back office,
the server on duty would be doing side work in the
kitchen, and until the bartender arrived at noon, I'd be
there at the host stand. Alone.

I pulled my phone out of my pocket. 6:50 a.m. I didn't
even bother trying to hold in the sigh that tumbled up
from my lungs. How was it possible for time to move so
slowly? I shoved my phone back in my pocket and steeled
myself to head back upstairs. Self-consciously, I tugged
down the cuffs of my suit jacket. A reflex. Almost. The
bandages weren't showing, or at least I had no reason to
think they were. Still, I needed to adjust. To conceal. "I'll
see you later, man."

"Laters, Gabe." Stanley's brow softened, and he
averted his gaze with a half smile. Was it sympathy? Pity?
Disgust? I tried not to dwell on it, climbed back into the
elevator, and pushed the button that would take me back
up to the thirteenth floor. But as I rode the elevator up,
floor by floor, my thoughts remained below. It occurred to
me that the look on Stanley's face very well may have been
fear.

Had people always been so freaked out by this place, and I never noticed? Or could it be that, following my time away from here, given the reasons for my absence, I was projecting my own anxieties about returning here onto my coworkers? My therapist would probably vote for the latter. But he wasn't here, and I couldn't be sure which idea I found more disconcerting.

Chapter Three

By the time the elevator arrived back at the thirteenth floor, it was 6:55. Breakfast service began at seven, and typically, the first server got here right around then. So, it made sense to not prop open the doors until a server arrived. Maybe if we had guests looking to get in first thing, but that never happened. It made more sense to leave the doors closed until we officially started serving people. Yet, no matter how hard I tried, I couldn't get Leslie to agree.

As I stepped off the elevator into the foyer, I could see the doors had been propped wide open like the arms of the creepy uncle your parents forced you to give a hug at family gatherings. The worst kind of welcoming. Unavoidable. It was a sign that Leslie had arrived.

I made my way to the host stand, relieved to note that my manager was nowhere to be seen. To the right of the entrance, a vintage oaken coat rack stood expectantly. Staff was under strict instruction to never actually hang coats on it. It was purely aesthetic. While complimentary coat check was available for guests and staff were expected to stow our jackets downstairs in the staff locker room, some of the management actively chose to ignore this directive. Looking now, I could see Leslie's signature puke-green peacoat hanging from the coat rack. She was definitely here.

I had two options. The first, I could continue my opening host duties. I could proceed to compile the VIP and allergy lists for the day's reservations, continue straightening place settings in the empty dining room, and guarantee myself a run-in with Leslie. Or option two, I could duck into the kitchen, grab myself a coffee from the server's station, and run out the clock until seven when Kelly, the server scheduled to work the breakfast shift, arrived.

Swinging open the kitchen door, I made my way to the server's station. From this end of the kitchen, the heavy black door of the back office seemed to be miles away. A sprawling, noisy expanse of kitchen stood between where I was and the far closet of an office Leslie had tucked herself away in. The kitchen shone: all white linoleum, chrome, and tile.

Even with the skeleton crew required for a Monday-morning breakfast shift, the kitchen was increasingly busy with activity and noise. The radio had begun to blare *Ranchera* music in Spanish, and I smiled to myself. I stepped behind the bulk of the espresso machine that created a natural barrier between the server station and the rest of the kitchen. Now that the kitchen staff had brought some life into the restaurant's back-of-house, being in there was like a breath of fresh air.

Aside from the delicious aromas and the beautiful white noise of chopping and stirring, the energy of the kitchen was different from the dining room. Here, I could breathe. Here I didn't have to have a smile permanently affixed to my face. I didn't have to have the soft, accommodating, ready-to-please voice of a host. Here I could be a person.

Pouring myself a cup of coffee from the large, heavy urn next to the espresso machine, I listened to the line cooks and prep chefs chat away in Spanish. They joked with one another and shared stories of their weekends. I could understand most things, but my Spanish wasn't good enough for me to contribute much.

"*Hola, muchacho.*"

"Shit!" I wasn't expecting the voice that addressed me from beyond the espresso machine. I jumped, startled, splashing a jet of hot coffee across my hand.

"*Lo siento! Cuidado, muchacho!*" Concerned, Sofia, one of the line cooks, stepped into the server area. "You okay?" With all the efficiency of an individual whose career revolved around the handling of things both hot and sharp, Sofia handed me a clean white rag from the front pocket of her equally clean white apron.

"*Gracias.*" I took the rag and wiped the hot liquid from the back of my hand. "I'm good, sorry. You just startled me." I laughed. Sofia was nice. I had known her since she started working in the kitchen maybe five months ago.

"*Lo siento.* I didn't mean to scare you." She seemed almost embarrassed. "Chef told me to ask how many covers we have today."

"Right. I'll check and let him know when I bring over the VIP list. *Gracias.*" I handed back the rag.

"*Y tu mano?*"

"*Está bien, gracias. Mira.*" I showed her my hand. It was a little red, but I'd survived worse. She looked at my hand, satisfied, but then, her expression shifted slightly. Her eyes were lingering but not on my hand. In extending my arm to show her I was all right, I had stretched out enough for the bandage on my wrist to emerge from my sleeve. I put on my best customer service smile and adjusted my cuffs. "*Y tú? Cómo estás, Sofia?*"

She must have realized she'd been staring and rushed to meet my eyes with hers. "*Tú sabes. Estoy aquí.* I'm here." She said this with a matter-of-factness that didn't quite qualify whether that was a good thing or not.

Sofia was kind. A hard worker with a good attitude. Every now and then, she would make an extra order of hash browns or bacon and set them aside in the server station for me. I remember chatting with her when she first started. She was so grateful for this job even though it was hard. She had come over from Mexico not that long before. Finally joining her husband in Chicago after a long period of separation courtesy of the US's fucked-up immigration policy.

"*Segura?* Is everything okay?" A glint similar to what I'd been seeing in the eyes of my coworkers all morning long flitted across her eyes. An uneasiness. Was it just around me? Had people been talking about the reasons for my absence? Had something gone down while I was gone? "Did something happen?"

Sofia didn't say anything for a long moment. The din of the kitchen beyond us now seemed far away.

"*Que pasó?*"

"*Nada. Nada más que lo normal.*" It was at this point which she burst into tears. I looked around, at a bit of a loss, as if the espresso machine would know what to do. Hesitantly, I put my arms around her. Her tears began to soak my shirt almost immediately. At her height, her face was right at my sternum. "You shouldn't have come back." Maybe it was the vibrations of her voice with her lips so close to my chest, but her words made my heart stutter.

"*Mande?*" I couldn't bring myself to look down at her,

instead asking the question to the rack of dishes and coffee cups. I could feel Sofia pull away, feel her look up at me, silently imploring me to meet her gaze. I finally did.

"You shouldn't have come back." Her voice was soft yet firm.

My two-week leave of absence, as referred to by management, had officially ended about a week ago. This was my first shift back on the schedule. Something definitely seemed different. People were more high-strung. This place had always hummed at a weird frequency. If I really thought about how best to put it, all morning there'd been the sensation that this weird frequency was being amplified.

I could see it in the faces of my coworkers if I looked closely enough. Strained expressions. Tension. The porters I'd seen, Stanley, Ernesto, and now Sofia. They were all skittish. So far, I'd taken it as a sign of awkward tension. Some of them knew why I had been gone, and those that didn't, I'm sure had heard rumors. Of course, people were acting weird. What is the "normal" way to engage with someone returning to the job following a suicide attempt?

"*Mira, Sofia, estoy bien. Estoy mejor. No te preocupes.*" For a moment, her concern was touching. Then I noticed the look on her face. She wasn't concerned for me. Or rather, she was but not for my mental well-being.

"*No. No me entiendes...* It's being here. *Aquí, este lugar.* This is a bad place." Her face, her voice all seemed to say that her concern had to do with my presence here, now; not with how close I came to being nowhere at all. The thought made me want to cry. I refused.

"Is this about Ceci? It's sad that she got fired, but...

Mira, Cecilia wasn't happy working here. I mean, none of us are *happy* here, *pero...*"

"No!" she repeated. This time her voice was free of any tears. The watery earnestness she had spoken with when I took her, crying into my arms, had evaporated into a clear, crystalline conviction. "Ceci was right. *Debemos salir. Todos nosotros deber salir...pero...* I can't. I need this job. *No tengo otras opciones. Necessito el dinero...no puedo salir.*"

Whether or not Cecilia was right when she said there was evil here, Sofia definitely was when she said she couldn't leave. She *couldn't*. She needed this job. The sort of work visas so many immigrants need in order to stay in the US require certification of employment, and changing the employer on all those documents was expensive, time-consuming, and complicated. She was stuck. And she knew it.

"*No puedo salir,*" she said again. Her voice was almost surprised. It was as if she had only just then realized this about her circumstances. I don't know if it was with a sense of acceptance or resignation, but she got very still. Using the sleeves of her white chef's frock, she wiped the tears from her face and straightened her spine. Her warm brown eyes had the look of polished hardwood. Strong and unbending.

"*Pero, tú te puedes. No lo olvides.*" With that, she headed back to her duties prepping the kitchen for the impending breakfast shift.

I grabbed my coffee and walked carefully back to the dining room. It had already started to cool. Gingerly, I took a sip as I walked, making sure not to spill. I arrived back at the host stand and made it a point to place my coffee squarely on the octagonal coaster that bore the

Rosebriar Room's insignia.

Powering up the iPad with the hosting software on it, I pulled out a paper copy of the same chart I filled out every day with its long table of information to be filled in. How many reservations were on the books. The names of any VIPs planning to dine with us. Food allergies, party sizes, table assignments, the projected times at which we'd be hit with rushes of hungry patrons. I went through the morning, reservation by reservation, listing this information as efficiently as I could so I'd be able to get it to Chef and the kitchen staff before the morning really got rolling.

Overhead, the restaurant's carefully curated mood music started to pour from the speakers. The playlist never changed. I didn't even need to pay attention to know which '60s Brit pop one-hit wonder would follow which hip cover by some indie-darling or another. As the Troggs began to warble about how "Love is All Around," I knew the music, controlled from the back office, was Leslie's way of saying that breakfast service had officially begun. I looked at my phone. The digital zero of 7:00 flitted to read 7:01.

Taking a breath, I tried to calm myself. I made an effort to release the tension I was holding in my shoulders and neck. Without fully understanding why, the weight of heavy anticipation sank in the center of my gut. But anticipation of what?

The hosting software informed me that our first reservation wasn't until nine thirty. The music lightened the atmosphere in the restaurant, at least partially, but the idea of standing here, more or less alone, for the next two and a half hours sounded like torture. I could feel the noxious mix of boredom and dull, consistent dread drifting my way, like a storm cloud on the horizon.

Out of habit, I started fiddling with my phone. A swipe, a poke, and a scroll with my finger across the smooth, inky, black glass of my screen, and before I realized it, I found myself on Kenny's Facebook page. He'd updated his profile picture. It was a picture of him and his dog, Leia. God, I missed that dog. God. I missed that man. My grip on my phone tightened, and the tips of my fingers started to redden with the pressure. I could feel my pulse behind my eyes and stinging in my wrists. Finally, with a click, the screen of my phone went black, and I stuffed it back in my pocket. My breathing was labored, heavy. I felt as if I had run up a flight of stairs, and the edges of my vision blurred and glowed. There was a tightening in my chest. A weight in the pit of my stomach that threatened to sink me to my knees.

At the edge of my peripheral vision, I caught a glimpse of a figure. In the corner of the room. Near the bar. The shadow of a man. I blinked, and he was gone. If he had been there at all. I swung my head in that direction. There was no man. The restaurant was empty and still. I was alone. Utterly alone.

In frustration, I slammed my hand down on the surface of the host stand harder than I meant to. The impact hurt. It felt good. I did it again. Three quick, hard slams of my fist against the hardwood of the host stand. "Shit!" A warmth started to spread at my wrist, and I squeezed my eyes shut, willing myself to calm down.

How could I be so stupid? Looking at Kenny's Facebook was masochistic and immature. I hated myself for being so weak. Hating myself had kind of become par for the course over the past couple of months since Kenny and I had split. I focused on breathing. In and out. In. Out.

Deep and steady. But standing there with my eyes shut made me more and more nervous. Like being a child in a dark hallway, fumbling for the light switch.

I opened my eyes to the empty Rosebriar. I continued to breathe. In my head rang Sofia's voice, though my mind translated her words to English. *I can't leave,* she had said. *But you can. Don't forget that.*

"I can leave," I said to the empty room. *Don't forget that.* I gingerly brought my fingers to the bandages on my wrist, vaguely alarmed to see a thin red line start to seep through the gauze. I could leave. Maybe it would be better if I did forget. Leaving isn't always the best option.

Chapter Four

The thin crimson line tentacled its way up the white cotton of the gauze bandage around my right wrist. "Dammit." I hadn't brought any fresh bandages with me. Realistically, if I actually needed to, I could take advantage of one of the well-stocked first aid kits tucked away behind the bar and at designated spots in the kitchen. My stitches had been removed about a week ago, so there weren't any left to pop.

After a second, the bright length of red stopped expanding. The sharp flash of pain that had flared when I slammed my hand down on the host stand started to subside. It still hurt, but less so: the secondary twinge of a healing wound. I rushed to make sure I hadn't sprung a leak on the left side too. All clear. Clean, soft white gauze. The steel anchor of my bracelet caught the light and twinkled. I tugged down the sleeves of my suit coat and grabbed the long-nosed lighter from the drawer. I made my way out from behind the host stand.

Seat by seat, I moved along the edge of the bar, lighting the little votive candles dotting the length of it. For a morning shift, with all the light spilling in through the east-facing windows, along with the various carefully adjusted lighting fixtures, the votives served absolutely zero purpose. But Leslie liked them.

I looked again at her coat hanging from the rack. What was it about this habit of hers that drove me nuts?

The fact that she considered herself the exception to the rule? Why should she be able to hang her shit on a coat rack the general manager had said was off-limits to *everyone*? Why should she be able to text on the floor and then turn around and write up a server for using their cell phone to check the time? She shouldn't. She did. I guess a lot of people do shit they shouldn't.

The morning playlist continued to cycle through its meticulously selected repertoire. Placebo's "Protect Me From What I Want" floated from the speakers, and I arrived at the end of the bar. Hanging on the wall above the bar's end was a tapestry. Whether it was actually old or just styled to look that way, I couldn't tell. An intricate floral-brocade pattern was woven into the border of it, and the tapestry itself was a Renaissance-looking depiction of Cain and Abel, muscle-bound and grappling, midfratricide.

Absentmindedly, I started adjusting the place settings, straightening the sparkling silver knives and forks and moving the crystalline water glasses ever so slightly to the precise correct angle in relation to the plates. After each, my eyes were drawn back to this tapestry. It was hypnotic. I could feel the cool glass in the palm of my hand, but my gaze was fixed on the stone in Cain's.

"Gabe!" Leslie's shrill voice shouted my name from the doorway of the kitchen, cracking like a whip through the dining room. Startled, I inadvertently let the glass in my hand crash to the floor. The noise of its shattering against the freshly polished hardwood made me wince and prompted Leslie to scream my name again. "Gabe! Come the fuck on! We haven't even had our first cover of the day, and you're breaking shit. Get it together."

Before I could respond, she retreated back into the kitchen, leaving me alone to clean up the mess. Adrenaline pumping, I looked around at the shards of glass strewn across the floor. "Goddammit." I set out to grab a broom.

I hate the mornings. I am not a morning person. So, I was pissed when I started getting scheduled for these opening shifts. The fact that I had to work with Leslie made it all the worse.

As she reemerged from the kitchen, scone in one hand and coffee in the other, I prepared myself to deal with her bullshit. After months of morning shifts with her, I had almost learned to accept her drawling sarcasm. Almost. But after being gone for over two weeks, I anticipated it taking me some time to readjust. "So, Mr. Espinosa, how many do we have on the books?"

"As of right now, fifty-five. First reservation isn't until nine thirty. Last rezo is for one thirty." I corralled the shards of glass into the bright-copper dustpan we usually kept tucked behind the garbage cans.

"Only fifty-five? Fuck me. Why do I even bother to come in?" Pulling out her phone to check the time, she sighed heavily. "Well, that's Monday for you, I guess."

"I guess."

"How are you holding up?"

"Been worse. You?"

"Great. Per yooj." Her abbreviation of the word "usual" made me smile. My best friend, Maisey, shared the habit. Though, while Maisey managed to make shortening words seem effortlessly cool, I couldn't say if I thought it was stupid or endearing when Leslie did the same.

"Have a good time at Rudy's?"

"Why? What did you hear?" she asked through a mouth full of scone.

"Nothing. I just know that y'all usually hit up Rudy's for the Sunday special."

"Oh. Right. It was a good time. It's too bad you never hang with us."

"Yeah, well my boyfriend...well, my ex, I mean, wasn't much of the Sunday-Funday type."

"Good thing you don't have to worry about that anymore then, huh?" She took a big gulp of coffee, oblivious.

I found myself flicking the steel anchor around my wrist back and forth. The motion of my hands must have drawn Leslie's gaze, and through the vague softness of her hangover, I registered something click into place behind her eyes. I could almost feel her processing an attempt at an apology.

"Gabe I, uh... I'm gonna head back to the office. Get some work done. I haven't seen Kelly yet, so on the off chance some hotel guest manages to crawl their ass up here looking for breakfast, I trust you can take care of them. Bitch better pray I don't write her ass up. I fucking hate tardiness."

I wanted to scream "Hypocrite!" in her face. Instead, I smiled and managed to make myself say softly, "Yeah, I can manage."

"Good. If some hungry fuck comes up here and ends up having to wait for Kelly's ass to show up and take their breakfast order, they'll end up dragging themselves over to Starbucks, and we'll be sitting here twiddling our fucking thumbs all morning. Wouldn't want that now, would we?"

As I looked into her eyes—still slightly glazed with the sheen of last night's booze—it took all my self-control to not hurl the glass filled dustpan in my hands to the floor right then and walk out. "No, Leslie. Of course not. I hate thumb twiddling."

Her skinny, pale face went blank for a second before bursting into a grin.

"Thumb twiddling." She guffawed. "That's right." Taking a crumbly bite from her scone, she headed back toward the kitchen and the manager's office beyond it. Over her shoulder she called, "Welcome back, by the way." And I was alone again.

In silence I finished sweeping up the glass and the spattering of scone crumbs Leslie had left in her wake. If today was like every other day, once she made her way back to the office, she'd promptly begin napping until the lunch rush hit.

With a sigh, I tried to shake off my frustrations. Things could always be worse. There were far worse jobs out there. Hell, I'd even had a few. I should be grateful. Especially as a twenty-seven-year-old who'd graduated into a job market freshly emerging from the dregs of the Great Recession. Considering the bachelor's degree I'd taken out thousands of dollars' worth of student-loan debt for was in communications, I should be even more grateful. My BA in communications, hardly the most useful of studies, definitely failed to qualify me for any high-paying positions straight out of undergrad. At least this hosting gig allowed me to support myself. It also saved me the indignity of having to move back to the suburbs with my parents. That was nothing to sneeze at.

I had to be grateful for my situation, I reminded myself as I emptied the dustpan into the garbage. I returned it along with the broom to their spot behind the bronze-plated trash cans that flanked the entryway.

"Excuse me, are you open for breakfast?"

"We are!" I said, startled. Normally, footsteps echo in the hallway, but I hadn't heard any sound from the speaker's approach, so the voice took me by surprise. I turned to face him only to make eye contact with one of the most beautiful people I had ever seen.

"Great, a table for one then," he said, his baritone voice hinting at a slight accent I couldn't place. Not quite French. Definitely European. Was it a Romance language? He was exceedingly well-dressed for seven in the morning, and his clothes said it all. Quality, stylish, but not overly fancy. He wore a well-tailored sport coat over a fitted sweater and a dress shirt underneath. All were coordinated with well-shined leather shoes and a matching belt. He wore the sort of clothes only worn by people with money. The sort that inspires both envy and appreciation.

"Of course. Follow me this way." Leading him into the otherwise empty restaurant, I tried my best to seem uninterested in his frustratingly good looks. Since it opened, the hotel had hosted its share of celebrities, not to mention various non-famous rich-and-beautiful people of all sorts. This guy made the hottest of them seem plain.

Grabbing a menu from the host stand, I walked to one of the nicer booths. "Are you a guest here at the hotel?"

"Yeah, in town for business. Lovely place." He moved through the space with a confident ease. He was put together as so many people who dined here tended to be. Monied. Refined. After a little while, you could spot them a mile away. The sort of folk who became regulars at a place where a standard meal could easily cost well into the triple digits.

"Yes. They did a good job renovating the place. Would you like some reading material? We've got *The Tribune, The Sun-Times—*"

"*The Tribune* would be great. Thanks."

"Of course." Working here had made dealing with privilege a well-honed skill. The privilege of money. The privilege of connections. The privilege of beauty. The privilege of whiteness. So many of the people who walked through the doors of the Rosebriar Room wore these privileges like a second skin. It made looking at them easier. No matter how stylish or beautiful, any lust or desire was muted by the fact that, while escorting them to their tables and offering newspapers, I might as well not exist. I was invisible to them. I was staff. The help. A nonentity.

I crossed away from his booth to the bar, feeling shabby in the H&M suit that was my uniform. I hated how easy it was for me to feel self-conscious and insecure. This stranger hadn't said or done anything to offend me, yet here I was, offended. As if it was this guy's fault I was drowning in student debt, suffering from low self-esteem, and hadn't been laid in a month and a half. Kenny and I had split a month ago, but there had been warning signs. If only I hadn't been too blind to see them.

"Here you are. Can I get you started with anything to drink?"

"Coffee, please. Black."

"Coming right up."

Moving away from him, I caught a whiff of his cologne. Smokey and sweet. The smell of bonfires and bourbon. I found myself smiling and forced myself to move from the table. I wondered if he was watching as I walked away. Was he looking at me like I'd been looking at him? I hoped he was. There's no better short-term cure for insecurity than a little attention. I managed to resist the urge to turn back and check until I reached the POS and entered in his drink order.

There was still no sign of Kelly. Generally speaking, morning shift was pretty dull, and strolling in a bit after seven was the norm for most of the servers. Even arriving as late as fifteen minutes wasn't unheard of. Servers were late all the time. Hosts didn't have that luxury. One coffee. Black.

Adjusting my hair, I looked up in the direction of the guy's booth. He was looking at me. More accurately, he was staring at me. His stare was direct. So much of life as a gay man hinges on the ability to read people. The fun and frustration of navigating interactions with other men. Making eye contact, flirting. The unspoken language of mutual desire. Seeing who does or doesn't belong to the same tribe, who speaks the same unspoken language. The sort of secret kinship of people who move through the world as the other, who need to identify one another in a sea of the status quo. The wordless interaction that indicates a man might be interested in you. Or might want to hurt you.

This man wanted to hurt me. I knew it somehow. Some part of me sensed it. I could see it in his eyes as they focused on me. I'd been on the receiving end of such looks before. Holding a lover's hand in the wrong neighborhood. Being a Mexican guy in the wrong part of the country. This man, who had just a moment ago seemed a calm, polite hotel guest, in an instant transformed into something volatile.

He hadn't moved since I'd walked away from him. He sat there, still except for his breathing which had become heavy. In and out. His shoulders rose and fell as his nostrils flared. All the while, his eyes never left mine. Never blinked.

"Sir? Are you okay?"

He said nothing in response. Then, gradually, his mouth split into a wide grin. I could see his perfect smile stretch and stretch. A white gash across his face. I could hear his teeth grinding against one another. It was a hard sound like marbles being jostled against one another. His jaw was tense. Rigid.

It was as though time had begun to crawl. Like my blood had thickened, and the air had thinned. I was afraid. What had changed? Had I done something to anger this man?

Without removing his eyes from me, with a slow, obscene grace, he rose from the booth. I didn't have to think about it. My body instinctively started backing away from this stranger. As if he were a rabid dog I had stumbled upon in an alley, he approached, and I withdrew. There were maybe seven feet between us. Making my way backward through the restaurant, I maintained those seven feet.

"Sir, I don't know what's happening here, but I need you to—to—to calm down. Okay? Just have a seat, and I'll call someone to help. Okay, I don—don't, I don't think you're well. Sir?" The words tumbled from my mouth, filling the air as I inched my way backward.

I couldn't take my eyes off this man. I couldn't blink. It was as though my gaze was the only thing keeping him from lunging across the space between us. I wanted to call out for help. Would the kitchen staff hear me from all the way out here? Would they even be able to hear me over the restaurant's music, their own radios, and the clanging pots and pans?

The rising sun shone through the glass-paned wall of windows that closed off the dining room from the terrace. I could feel the heat of it on my back as I neared the edge of the room. The entryway to the restaurant lay beyond the man, and our halting dance continued to push us further and further away from both the entrance and the door to the kitchen.

There was an emergency stairwell along the far wall just beyond the banks of the two-top tables we had been making our way past. With the space between us, we were each equidistant from the door marked Fire Exit in red. It would be a gamble to see which of us would make it there first.

At first glance, this man was in great shape. I'd been a runner since high school and might be able to beat him to the door, but being at least five inches taller than me, he had the advantage of longer legs. A longer stride. That could make all the difference. It wasn't the sort of gamble I was looking to make.

For a split second, I shifted my eyes to the stairwell door. That was enough. Before I even had the chance to decide to go for it, he leapt across the table between himself and the exit and then spun to face me with his mad grin. The sudden movement triggered an instinctive response in me, and I rushed forward as well. My hands slammed to the tabletop, and I braced myself. He'd read my intention and cut off my escape route.

Frantically, my fingers scrambled to lift one of the silver knives from its precisely adjusted place setting. Extending the blade out before me, I desperately wished I hadn't listened to Leslie when she repeatedly told me to stow my phone away in the host stand.

"Why are you doing this?" Instead of the authority I'd hoped to hear in my voice, there was only fear.

"This is only the beginning." The man's smooth baritone had been replaced with a deep, guttural bass. A voice that was entirely different from the one he'd ordered coffee with only moments before. It was the voice of a wholly different person. The handsome features I'd found so striking had contorted into a face twisted with hate and sick pleasure. From behind his wide, toothy grin, a laugh rooted in his throat—humorless and croaking—filled the air between us. I tightened my grip on the knife.

On the far side of the restaurant, the door to the kitchen swung wide. Kelly, tying her apron around her waist, strolled into the dining room oblivious to the standoff happening at the other side of the restaurant. "7:05 on the dot. Only five minutes. Leslie can't tell me shit!" Then, she registered the two of us across the room. "What the fuck?"

With the man's attention temporarily drawn away from me, I made a break for the emergency exit. Before I had time to comprehend what was happening, the man broke into a sprint. In a desperate attempt, I used the full weight of my body to shove one of the heavy tables into his path. Moving only a margin of inches, the table slid toward him. With a growling laugh, he grabbed the obstruction by its thick oaken tabletop. The sound of splintering wood filled the air as his fingers dug into the oak, and he proceeded to do the impossible. Grinning like a madman, he lifted the thing over his head. The solid-wood tabletop had a bronze-plated, metallic base that easily weighed close to three hundred pounds. This man lifted it over his head with as much effort as I might lift a moderately sized bag of groceries.

Kelly shrieked from the kitchen doorway, drawing his attention once more. He twisted his body to face her without reorienting his feet, grotesquely contorting the angles of what should be anatomically possible. Every instinct I had was telling me to rush through the exit, to run down those stairs as fast as I could, and not look back, but I couldn't. Not when Kelly stood there frozen.

There was a faraway look in her eyes. She was rooted to the spot, mouth hanging open like a dresser drawer hastily left agape. I could see her, struggling to understand what she was seeing. In my mind, I could see this man hurling a table at her. I could hear her bones crunching under its weight. I could imagine her getting crushed like a bug: the cracking, the wet sounds, the screams, the pain.

"Hey!" I shouted, rushing back toward the middle of the room. "Leave her alone!"

Like some horrific, man-sized windup toy from hell, the man spun back to face me and launched the table in my direction. In a split second, I had to register what happened. My mind leapt to images of the shot putters from my high school track team. Miraculously, while my eyes were occupied with flying tables and my mind with high school athletes, by the grace of God, my body was entirely in the moment. Some small, mammalian part of my brain engaged, and at the last moment, I managed to scurry out of the way just as the table crashed through the Tiffany-glass doors of the terrace. He had launched the thing with such force it shot to the dead center of the patio and, with an almost cartoonish, cracking bounce, flipped over the railing at the edge of the balcony. The table flew into the chasm of morning sky beyond the thirteenth floor of the hotel.

With a manic laugh, the stranger roared, his head leaning back until the back of his scalp was nestled between his shoulder blades. And then there was silence. He hung there, balancing on his tiptoes like a lost contortionist. And then he crumpled to the ground.

Kelly and I stared in silence at the shards of glass, the terrace in disarray, and the quivering, now pathetic, mass of a man on the floor. The music played on, hollow and tinny, as my pulse pounded in my ears. A dull ache in my hand made me look down and notice I was still holding the knife. Gripped so tightly in my fist, the silver had started to dig painfully into the flesh of my palm. After what seemed like forever, I registered the sound of a collision from the street below. Screams and sirens cried out from far away.

Chapter Five

Red. Blue. Red. Blue. The lights of the emergency vehicles flickered back and forth, washing the sidewalk in red and blue as the police officers asked me questions. It was chilly, sitting at the lip of an open ambulance down on Michigan Avenue. At some point, someone had given me a blanket. I couldn't remember who. The faces of everyone but that man as he lay crumpled on the ground had become a blur in my mind.

From where I sat now, I could see the point of impact where the table had crashed into the ground. A mass of splinters and cracked pavement. It was a miracle no one had died. Falling icicles killed pedestrians in Chicago often enough to warrant yellow warning signs every spring. I mentally tried to drum up some statistics about fatalities from falling tables. Any distraction that might serve to keep that man's face from my mind would do. But his impossibly wide smile still flashed in my head.

"Sir? I know this is hard, but could you answer the question?"

Detective Hendricks looked at me expectantly. I had completely missed her asking the question. I was caught in a loop, recalling the EMTs carting away the man on a stretcher. He'd been unresponsive. They had piled him into an ambulance and rushed him away as more and more officials arrived on the scene. A scene in which I had somehow found myself center stage.

I could feel the detective's eyes on me. She was trying to be patient and had succeeded through all my stuttered responses and fractured retelling of events, but I could sense that whatever patience she had was starting to wear thin. Her professionalism could only hold out so long.

From the corner of my eye, I noticed Leslie and Kelly speaking to officers as well. Across the distance I could hear Leslie, shrill and anxious, "I already told you! I was in the back office. I don't know!"

The chill of the November morning sliced through my cheap suit. Numb, I pulled the blanket around me tighter. "I'm sorry, could you repeat the question?"

"I asked if you had ever met Len Starkey before today."

"I, I don't know who that is."

Detective Hendricks let out a sigh before flipping through a few pages in a palm-sized, black-leather notebook.

"Len Starkey, twenty-eight. In town from Stockholm, Sweden. He was in Chicago for business and a guest here at the hotel. He's the man who allegedly attacked you."

The detective wasn't wearing a uniform. Instead, she had on a charcoal suit and white blouse. Practical. Clean. Her thick, dark hair was piled neatly in a bun on the back of her head. A mild wave of relief washed over me as I realized I'd be dealing with a Black, female officer. Out of uniform. The thought of dealing with one in their blues made me queasy. Cops made me nervous. White, male cops in particular; ever since one followed me into my own backyard when I was ten. He'd evidently been suspicious of a brown kid running between the homes of a predominately white suburb. My mother had asked me to take out the trash while I was in the middle of watching my favorite TV show, and I had raced to make it back inside before the commercial break ended. I don't think I ever caught the end of that episode of *Boy Meets World*.

Returning my attention to Detective Hendricks, I tried to focus. "I've never been to Europe."

"Excuse me?"

"He...the guy, you said he was from Stockholm? Sweden," I said, "I've never been."

"And you hadn't encountered him elsewhere? Around the hotel since he checked in last evening."

"No, ma'am. I'm sorry." She shut her notebook. "What was wrong with him?" I thought of how still and silent the man—Len Starkey, twenty-eight, of Stockholm, Sweden—had been when they carted him out of the Rosebriar. How his eyes had been frozen wide open. I had seen a tear, glistening like a stray shard of glass, slide down his cheek. His face had become a blank, expressionless mask. "I've never seen anything like that."

"We don't know. He's been unresponsive since authorities arrived on the scene. Once we get a hold of his medical records and process a tox-screening, we'll have a better idea of what happened." She looked at me. Curious. "Did anything happen between you two that morning? Anything that might have provoked him? Something you might have done or said, intentional or otherwise?"

I thought back to when he had first entered the restaurant. Had I looked at him too long? Did my gaze somehow trigger something in him? Was this all my fault? "I... I don't think so. Our interaction was brief. He came in, sat, and I gave him the paper and took his coffee order. It all happened so fast. I'm sure you can check the security video."

"We will. Thank you for your cooperation Mr. Espinosa." She pulled out a small business card holder from her pocket and from it retrieved a crisp, white rectangle which she proceeded to extend toward me. "If any other details come to mind, or you remember something you might find relevant, please don't hesitate to call."

"Thank you."

She made her way over to some uniformed policemen and huddled around the now-splintered table's point of impact. I offered a thankful nod to the EMTs hovering near the ambulance we'd been perched on, and leaving the blanket behind me, I made my way back to the hotel.

Cutting straight through the marble tiled foyer, I pushed my way through the fire door marked Private and headed downstairs toward the staff locker room. Once through the door, though, I had to stop. The fluorescent lights buzzed overhead, shining off the cold aluminum of the stairs. The locker room was down those stairs in the basement where the freshly painted, white cement walls seemed to stretch on forever. A rat's maze. Before I could force myself to start descending those stairs into the bowels of the hotel, I had to sit down. I could feel my pulse throbbing behind my eyes once more, could feel my chest constricting as it became harder to breathe. Above, the white lights flickered behind their frosted-plexiglass panels, and I could feel a wave of dizziness coming.

Bracing myself against the wall, I let myself slide down as the floor rose to meet me. I sat there, focusing all my energy on breathing, doing my best not to puke. Head between my knees, I continued breathing in and out until my vision stopped vibrating. In that moment, more than anything, I wanted—needed—to hear Kenny's voice. Instinctively, I reached for my phone. "Shit."

It took everything I had to climb to my feet and make my way to the service elevator, which would take me back up to the thirteenth floor. There, the elevator would slide open in the Rosebriar's kitchen like it always did. The thought of it, of going back up there, made me feel even more like throwing up. Still, I pushed the call button.

Beyond the steel doors, I could hear the rumblings of the elevator descending. As I stood there, fidgeting and impatient, waiting for the elevator to arrive, I saw it. Something. Just barely. Out of the corner of my eye. A flash of movement. I spun, forcing my back to the elevator. A smell hit my nose. Bourbon and bonfires. With a ding, the elevator arrived, its doors sliding open behind me.

"Gabe?" asked someone from within the elevator. The unseen speaker's voice took me completely by surprise. All the air in my lungs rushed out in a startled cry.

"Ahhh!" I stumbled to my knees, my hands groped along the dirty cement floor before me. As I gasped for air tears began to stream down my face.

"Gabe! Are you okay? Breathe, dude, breathe. You're okay. It's okay."

Kneeling, Rodney, the sous-chef from the Rosebriar, leaned toward me from the elevator. He seemed almost as freaked out as I was. Tentatively, he placed his hands on my shoulders, forcing me to make eye contact with him. The steadiness of his firm grip grounded me. I failed to resist a flash of embarrassment. A grown man, crumpled on the floor crying? Pathetic.

"I'm okay. Thanks, I'm okay." Using my sleeves, I wiped the tears from my face, eager to not seem like a total fucking mess. "Really, I'm fine." Chef Rod looked at me for a long moment. His hazel eyes studying my face, maybe trying to make sure I wouldn't lose my shit the moment he let me go.

"You sure?" His concern surprised me. Since I started working here, Rod and I had interacted fairly regularly, but I couldn't remember a time he'd actually used my name before. He had the sort of bad-boy, rock-star vibe so common among chefs; no matter how counterintuitive that might seem. He was all tattoos, bandanas, and a bad attitude. Before getting into the restaurant industry, I wouldn't have known such a cliché' even existed, but Chef Rod was a prime example. This made the gentleness of his expression all the more surprising.

"Yeah, thanks." Gradually, I rose to my feet.

Rod straightened himself, taking a step back. "So, no brunch service, I guess."

"Nope." It was obvious that neither of us knew what to say. I could practically feel his curiosity frothing beneath the surface. It occurred to me that everyone in the building must know what happened. To some degree, at least. They had the headline and would be looking to me for the rest of the story. The mere thought of recounting the morning's events to my coworkers left me unbearably exhausted. I shook it off, doing my best to steel myself against the fear and shock this morning had thrown my way. I needed to get the fuck out of this place. "You just come from up there? I left my phone in the host stand. Are they letting people in? I really need to get the hell out of here. Think I'll be able to grab it?"

"I dunno, probably? It seems like they were wrapping things up. You sure you wanna go back up there? After..."

"Absolutely not." Despite saying so, I forced myself into the elevator. The doors began to close, and I took a deep breath. Before they shut, Rod stuck his hand between them, triggering them to reopen. Joining me in the elevator, he gave me a nod. The doors shut behind him. "Thanks."

"Don't mention it. You look scared as shit." A laugh barked from my mouth, surprising me almost as much as Rod. After a second, he started laughing too. "God, millennials and their phones." This prompted more laughter from the both of us, and we made our way back up to the thirteenth floor. Back up to the Rosebriar Room.

The green, glowing numeral above the button panel ticked away as the elevator took us past each floor. Fifth floor, sixth floor, seventh floor. It took a conscious effort to keep breathing. Our laughter had subsided, and the two of us stood there in silence until, finally, a metallic ding announced our arrival. The doors slid open, and beyond them, the white-and-chrome kitchen loomed: empty and still. "Come on."

When after a moment I still hadn't started to move, Rod's impatience wore through whatever pity had inspired him to treat me so gently. "Are you fucking kidding me?" I had no words. My mind's eye had started to replay the events of that morning. I couldn't step out of that elevator. I was like a scared child, embarrassed by my foolishness.

Rod sighed, shaking his head with a sharp bark of a laugh. I wasn't sure if he was laughing at my cowardice or at himself for thinking I might be anything other than useless. Chefs generally didn't think particularly highly of front-of-house staff. With a roll of his eyes, he tucked a strand of his long, stringy brown hair behind his ear. "Wait here. The host stand?"

I nodded, again surprised by his kindness, and he stepped off the elevator.

All our interactions up to this point had consisted of disinterested exchanges about guest counts and food allergies. I remember one incident when, after a food runner failed to show up for his shift, I got roped into helping carry food out to the tables. As inexperienced as I was at balancing the ceramic ramekins, sauciers, and plates on my arms, he'd lost his patience and sent me back to the host stand, preferring to be short-staffed than deal with my incompetence. I remember cursing him and his stupid bandana under my breath for the rest of the shift.

After a moment or two alone in the elevator with my thoughts, Rod's voice rang out, "Gabe!" With a soft *whoosh*, my phone sailed through the air from where he stood in the kitchen. Unexpecting and clumsy, I let the phone hit me square in the chest, and it slipped through my fumbling fingers to the floor. "Wow. Really?"

"Sorry," I mumbled, unsure why I was apologizing. Reentering the elevator, Rod pressed the button. The doors slid shut with a crash and our descent began. I gazed down at the phone at my feet, remembering why I had so desperately needed the damn thing in the first place. I'd been dying to call Kenny. It had become a habit: when anything happened, large or small, my first instinct was to tell him everything. I had grown so used to sharing all the little mundanities of my daily life with him. Texting throughout the day, stupid little jokes and goofy animated GIFs; upon breaking up with him, I found myself struggling to resist the urge like a smoker going it cold turkey. I almost wanted to just leave the stupid phone there on the floor. Instead, I knelt to grab it. Distracted, I didn't notice Chef Rod doing the same.

Rod had a well-documented record of slutting it up with various female staff members at the Rosebriar. I had enjoyed the reports of numerous female servers and bartenders after they'd had their go with Chef Rod. I'd also bitten my tongue as he lobbed the word "gay" around the kitchen like a dodgeball; a teasing bro-ism hurled at various members of the kitchen staff. I'd even shaken my head and clucked disapprovingly as some of the other gay guys on staff had admired Rod from afar. Sure, he was rakishly handsome in the usual, frustrating way, but I refused to waste my time and energies on a flirty straight boy. After so many sociology and human sexuality courses in undergrad, I knew enough to fight the internalized homophobia that made the scruffy, macho bad-boy chef so appealing. But it had been a long fucking morning.

The two of us knelt there on the floor of the elevator for a moment that seemed to stretch longer than it could have possibly been. I was caught by surprise as his fingertips inadvertently grazed mine. As a general rule, I'd try to quash any flirting with a known straight guy, but I was too tired for any high horse. Instead, I let my eyes meet his. I didn't withdraw my hand. Normally, I would abruptly pull away in one of those countless "No homo"s intended to put the ever-skittish straight boys at ease. Instead, I let the touch linger.

On the panel, the green numerals ticked down past the floors. Seventh floor, sixth floor, fifth floor. He didn't avert his eyes. He didn't withdraw his touch. We kneeled there over my phone, floating in stasis, his face was barely an inch or two from mine. And just like that, the inch or two disappeared. I didn't think about it. Couldn't think about it.

His lips were softer than I expected, and the scruffiness of his constant five-o'clock shadow scraped satisfyingly against my clean-shaven face. His hand, firm and slightly calloused, landed on the nape of my neck, drawing me in. Then, with a ding, the elevator announced our arrival at the lower level.

I hadn't realized I had closed my eyes until they sprang open. Closing my fingers around my phone, I stood sharply and shot through the still-opening doors of the elevator. Without looking back, I headed straight for the staff exit. Lips still tingling, I shouted over my shoulder, "Thanks for grabbing my phone."

Chapter Six

What the fuck? What the fucking fuck? I sat there on the Blue Line, making my way home, unable to think anything else. "What the fuck?"

"Excuse me?" The elderly woman sitting across the aisle from me did not look amused. I hadn't realized I'd spoken the words aloud until she responded. Heat collected in my ears as embarrassment sent all the blood rushing to my head, and I tried to smile apologetically. With a scowl, she pulled her folding cart closer to herself, fussily rustling the plastic grocery bags it contained. She looked at me suspiciously.

"Sorry." I pulled out my phone in a vain attempt to seem less like a crazy person. A small blue LED light blinked away in the corner of the phone's face, telling me I'd received a new voice mail. I hadn't noticed it ring. It hadn't vibrated or anything since I'd left Rod in the elevator, and I knew I'd checked it as I walked away from the Sentinel Club. But to be fair, my mind had evaporated into a disoriented cloud as the course of the morning's events continued to unfold. The fact that I could recognize the object in my hand as a phone at all was probably a blessing.

I activated the screen with a swipe of my finger, waking up the dark rectangle of the phone's display to reveal my screen's wallpaper: a mural on the wall of a Logan Square coffee shop near my apartment. It was a squirrel in a luchador mask, biting into a heart instead of an acorn. Not too long ago, it had been a picture of Kenny, Leia, and me.

I swiped a lazy letter L into the dotted matrix that made up my phone's lock screen. Sure enough, a notification popped up, showing the new voice mail icon. The contact information indicated it was from the Rosebriar Room. It must be Leslie, of course, with some information about when we'd be resuming service. Or maybe it was Rod. Why would he be calling me? To apologize? To ask me out? To fire me? Could he fire me?

My heart fluttered, confused. Did I want it to be him calling? Was I ready for something like that? Why would my mind leap to such conclusions if part of me didn't want it to be Rod's voice in my mailbox? What a fucking mess. Increasingly tired, I clicked the icon. But as the voice mail began to play, it wasn't Leslie's bored voice I heard coming from my phone. Instead it was the voice of a man. Definitely not Rod. A faintly accented baritone sunken into a guttural bass. I recognized it instantly.

It was the voice of the man from that morning; not the genteel, coffee-ordering voice of a man from Sweden, but the roughened growl of a man transformed. A voice torn from a throat that had been screaming. My blood ran cold. I could feel it, icy in my veins. "This is only the beginning." His laugh, humorless, croaking, and raw, echoed in my head. "Be seeing you, Gabe. Soon."

The white gash of his smile. The deadened eyes locked on me. The grinding teeth. It couldn't be him. I had seen him carted off to Northwestern Memorial. He was practically catatonic. After his episode, or whatever you might want to call it, he hadn't been able to move, let alone make a phone call. The man had survived. I knew that. I had been told as much. But how would he get my phone number? How would the call say it was coming from the restaurant? How would the police let this man contact me? So many questions hurdled through my brain as the train hurdled its way through the tunnels of the underground tracks. There was no way.

The message ended, but I continued to sit there, the phone pressed to my cheek. The smooth glass of the screen lay cold against my face. The woman across the aisle narrowed her eyes at me. Her glare was sharp enough to cut. A tightening in my face informed me that the corners of my mouth had curled into a smile. Apologetic. A customer service smile. The smile of a servant.

It's funny, or perhaps the opposite of funny, how muscle memory often takes over in strained social interactions. Inside, I was falling apart. The man from that morning's voice, his laugh, rolled around inside my head. A boulder crushing all the other thoughts I'd had. My lizard brain somehow managed to keep my heart beating and my lungs inflating and deflating, inflating and deflating, sounding loud in my ears. It managed to turn my numb face into the complacent, abiding visage that this random white woman sitting across from me might find tolerable; but beyond that, I might as well have been a corpse sitting there on the 'L.'

Cold and exposed, every sound hit my ears like a tornado siren. The fluorescent lights of the train car, the bright, cold fall sunshine, it all seemed too bright. *Be seeing you, Gabe. Soon.* This wasn't happening. I was losing it. There couldn't be any other explanation.

With great effort, I managed to relax the arm muscles that had tightened into stone and eased the phone down from my ear. I looked at it in my hand, my hand in my lap. Smooth and black like a mirror. My eyes looked back up at me from its reflective surface. They had an unhinged gleam that prompted a giggle to escape from my lips.

I could feel the woman's glare. "What?!" My voice snapped. "What do you want?!"

The whole train went silent. It wasn't particularly loud before, but real silence, tense silence stands out when compared to the casual quiet of murmurs and white noise that are so easily tuned out. Now, it wasn't just this one woman's eyes on me. I could feel the other commuters looking at me too like I was some kind of insect.

I looked down at my phone and promptly deleted the voice mail. If I listened to it again, I would lose my mind. I knew it. I could feel it. If I had to sit here and listen to that voice again, that laugh, my sanity would be lost. I knew it the same way I knew as a child, lying still in the darkness, that if I moved even an inch, the beast hiding beneath my bed would snap my neck like a twig.

The train lurched to a stop under me, and I stood abruptly. I rushed out onto the platform. It didn't matter which station we'd stopped at. I'd catch the next train if need be. I just needed to be off that car and away from those stares. By way of coincidence or muscle memory, the stop I was compelled to get off at was just the one I needed. I found myself looking up at the blue-and-gray sign reading Logan Square. Relief washed over me, and I trudged my way up the stairs to the street beyond, making my way toward my apartment.

Chapter Seven

Fragrant, green ivy crept up the face of my apartment building. It climbed over the red bricks and framed the yellow door, making the whole two-flat look like a fuzzy green giant. The morning air chilled the metal of the key in my hand as I shoved it into the door. Metal against metal, clicking and grinding as it, per usual, stuck midturn in the lock. "Come on, you stupid fucking thing. Please."

The shining glass panels leading to the building's entryway reflected the street. In the glass, I could see someone standing across the street behind me. It was the figure of a man. Or at least it looked like a man for the split second I was able to register the figure's reflection. I sucked in a gasp of air and spun to face the street. There was nothing there. "I'm losing it," I said aloud to the gray sky.

With a distinct click, my key finally turned in the lock, and I stumbled onto the landing of my apartment building. With the door closed behind me finally, I could breathe again. The glass door pressed against my back, unmoving in its frame. I twisted shut the deadbolt and switched the keys in my hand as I made my way to the next door, this one leading to the stairs that climbed up to my apartment on the second floor.

Beyond that door, stairs disappeared up into shadows. The alley-facing window that usually illuminates the stairwell from between our building and the next hadn't yet fallen into the still-rising sun's range. It didn't help that my roommate and I had failed to replace the single, dead light bulb hanging overhead. The one that the switch at the foot of the stairs ought to turn on.

I had climbed those stairs a million times. Drunk, sober, half asleep. They were a familiar and usually comforting indicator that I was home. That my bed was nearby. That rest was at hand. In the middle of the night, on numerous occasions, I had crawled my way up those stairs in the pitch-black dark. And now? I was frozen at the foot of them. Staring up into the gloom. Incapable to making my way up. I might as well have been at the bottom of a well.

O God, I have an ill-divining soul. Methinks I see thee now, thou art so low. As one dead in the bottom of a tomb. The words floated into my head like a whisper, descending from the dark at the top of the stairs. I didn't have to do it. I could give up right there. Curl into a ball at the foot of the stairs. I could let the shadows swallow me whole. I could close my eyes there and be done with it. Or I could find the will to climb the goddamn stairs.

After a moment's hesitation, I reached out my hand and pulled the door shut behind me. I turned the door's lock, sealing shut the foyer from the stairs that led up to my apartment. So many doors, so many locks. I began my ascent. Activating my phone, I used the glow of its screen to guide my way up the stairs. According to the clock, it was eight thirty. Around this time my roommate, Bryan—assuming he'd spent the night here and not in the bed of some random hookup—would be just heading out the door toward his own job. Otherwise, he'd be running around getting ready, in a late rush to do so. But when I reached the third and final door to my apartment, the one that waited at the top of the stairs, it was closed. There was no sound coming from the apartment beyond it. Bryan must have gotten lucky last night.

The silence froze my hand on the doorknob. It somehow left me feeling hollow. The prospect of opening this last door into the quiet of an empty apartment suddenly made me unbearably sad. It was the last thing I wanted to do. As tired as I was. As much as I wanted to just lie down and sleep off the madness of the morning, I couldn't bring myself to open the door.

I had called this apartment home since Kenny and I moved in here together a year and a half ago. We ended up renting the second room to Bryan in order to save some money. It was the place Kenny and I had made our home. When we split, it was the place that I had decided to stay. He didn't want it, so I kept it. Now it was *my* home, no longer ours. He'd found somewhere new.

Twisting the knob, I opened the door to the empty apartment. "Hello?" I called out, knowing I'd get no response. But I needed my voice to vibrate through the empty stillness of the apartment before I could bring myself to enter. "Fuck."

Alone, the weight of that morning's insanity came crashing down on me. I was tired. I hadn't slept well the night before, and waking up so early hadn't helped with the exhaustion. Given the day's course of events so far, I was surprised to find myself able to stand at all. A growl rustled in my gut. I was hungry too. Hungry, tired, and losing my mind, I chucked my keys down on the table and made my way toward the kitchen.

Throughout the apartment lunch were half-empty shelves. A half-empty closet. Weird blank spaces on the walls where Kenny had taken his family pictures with him, pulling them down when he left. The whole place was a testament to what ends up left behind after the singular life a couple builds together reverts to being two distinct ones.

Bryan kept most of his stuff cloistered into his small room at the back of the apartment. I'd always appreciated this fact for the sake of tidiness, but now, the sparseness of the place made it feel empty and aching. Where there was once Kenny's stupid fucking Jason Mraz poster, there was nothing. The corner that used to house Leia's dog bed was now empty. Maybe if some of Bryan's god-awful art were hanging there on the wall, or if his cast-iron dumbbells were stacked in the corner, it'd be less painful to see the apartment's emptiness. But no, Bryan kept his shit in his room. And being in the apartment left me feeling like I was walking through a looted mausoleum.

In the kitchen, I opened the fridge, looking for something, anything to stuff in my face before I passed out. Of course, on the shelves designated mine, there was nothing but a bag of old, stale, vaguely green tortillas. Moldy. I tossed them into the trash and kept looking. I could cook. I was capable of it. Good at following directions, I could whip up a mean meal if the occasion called for it. It had so rarely called for it recently, and I hadn't even bothered buying groceries.

I grabbed a package of lunch meat from Bryan's shelf in the fridge. Pulling it open, I scarfed down a couple of slices of turkey breast. I doubt Bryan would miss a couple pieces of meat. He had plenty.

Every other night Bryan would bring home a different companion. Men. Women. Sometimes I couldn't help but envy him. While most people were stuck fishing for a partner in one half or the other of the human population, Bryan didn't have to worry about that. But envying Bryan for being bisexual was pointless. It would be about as worthwhile as envying any of the inescapable masses of straight people I found myself endlessly surrounded by. It smacked of the internalized homophobia I was always trying to resist.

I was no stranger to envy. As a single man, I often envied, even resented the happy couples that floated around, oblivious. I envied the ease with which my coupled friends had found each other. I envied the ease with which white gays matched with their doppelgangers for their Instagram #CoupleGoals. Finding Kenny had been a welcome respite from the cloying jealousy I'd grown accustomed to. He was one of the first white guys I went on a date with that didn't call me "Papi" or seem overly excited to practice their Spanish on me.

Bryan, also white, never had to deal with that. When every app and dating site is saturated with white faces and profiles overtly listing preferences for other white men only, it was easy to find myself resenting Bryan. As much as I tried to resist the impulse, it would be a lie to say I didn't hold it against him to a certain degree. The apparent ease with which he could find someone to share his bed bothered me. Especially now that I'd been thrust back into the depths of my loneliness. I stuffed a few more slices of turkey into my mouth before tossing the container back into the refrigerator. I let the door slam shut behind me.

With a yawn, I trudged my way down the hall to my room. Somehow, I made it to my bed. The blankets and pillows on my side were still crumpled and sunken from where I tossed and turned the night before. The other half of the bed was still smooth and cool. Thinking of the bed in terms of halves, my side and his side, was another habit I would have to break, along with my reluctance to making the bed in the morning. Kenny had always been the one to do it. I'd never really seen the point.

I added my uniform blazer to the pile of dirty clothes that were strewn about the floor and collapsed onto the bed. With the little energy I had left, I kicked off my black dress shoes and rolled over onto my back. The emotional rollercoaster of that morning's events left me simultaneously exhausted and restless. I lay there, looking up at the ceiling. My mind brought forward that man's face, his eyes. Fear sank like a stone in my gut. Clenching my eyes shut, I tried to shift my attention.

The elevator. Rod, with his stupid fucking bandana. His stupid fucking name. His stupid fucking hands on my shoulders. Heavy and strong. I hardly knew the guy, despite having worked with him since I started at the Rosebriar. Half of our few encounters left me annoyed by his cockiness or bored with his attitude. The other half left me flicking him off from behind the host stand. But the memory of his lips on mine silenced the moaning dread that echoed in my mind. The manic, wide-eyed grimace of the stranger was replaced with Rod's concerned gaze. I didn't have to like him. A kiss was just a kiss. No more, no less. But still I found myself thinking of his hand on the nape of my neck, pulling our lips together all the tighter. The slip of his tongue in my mouth.

There in bed, I let the desperately needed distraction run its course. Clumsily unfastening my belt, I proceeded to let my hand slip under the band of my briefs. I allowed myself to imagine my hand was his, and when I was done, I picked up yesterday's T-shirt from the floor, cleaned myself off, and drifted into unconsciousness. It was a thick, muddy sleep. I only wish it had been devoid of dreams.

Chapter Eight

I knew it was a dream. I could feel it. It was like I was floating above myself. Watching as my body moved through the lobby of the Sentinel Club Chicago. There was nobody there, but I wasn't alone. I could feel eyes watching me from the shadows. I could hear the clink of glasses in the distance, of cheery male voices, tucked away in the depths of the hotel. A fire roared in the fireplace. I could hear my footsteps echo against the marble and tile and polished wood.

I had no control over my body. It walked as if in a trance through the foyer. I looked on, seeing myself stroll past the reception desk. Step by aching step, I ascended the marble staircase. As I reached the top, my perspective was wrenched from an ethereal floating into the heaviness of my body's weight. In the dream, my limbs became impossibly heavy. That's when I felt it.

Hot and wet, pouring down my hands. Dripping in a rush down my fingertips. Blood poured from my wrists. The bandages were swept away in a torrent as a tide of red flooded down my forearms, pooling on the polished white marble of the stairs. Like a waterfall, it cascaded from where I stood at the top of the stairs.

I gazed down at my hands, shining and red, and in this dream, I could feel myself grow cold. Every move and sensation and reaction seemed to take forever. Dream time was slow and molasses like. I looked up from my hands and realized that the twin statues of Adonis were looking directly at me. Their gazes, usually matched at each other from either side of the stairs, were now both fixed directly on me. I stood there staring, transfixed, as they descended from their pedestals. The grayish-blue veins of the marble seemed to pulse across their stone muscles, and they approached me from either side. Their usual stoic faces had been replaced in matching leers. Obscene smiles. While I was frozen in place at the top of the stairs, they moved, swift as sharks, until I could feel the chill emanating off the cool marble of their not-flesh. Their stone fingers reached out for me and then...nothing.

Everything seemed to fade to black. But in the darkness, I could hear laughter and crying. Through the thick haze of my dream's darkness, I recognized the crying as my own.

Chapter Nine

When I opened my eyes, hours had passed. I realized my face was wet. I had been crying in my sleep. Sleepily, I wiped the tears from my face and took a deep breath. The warm yellow light of the midday sun poured in through the windows of my bedroom, and the weight of Kenny in bed beside me made brought a smile to my face. With a yawn, I stretched, content until the smile on my face froze. After he picked up the last of his shit, Kenny left his keys on the dining room table. He hadn't been back since. He couldn't be the one lying next to me.

Dread seemed to fracture the instant into an eternity. The instinct to leap from the bed slammed against the need to roll over and see who had sidled next to me while I slept. The impact of these two conflicting impulses left me paralyzed. I lay there immobilized. It was almost as though I could feel the blood rushing just below the surface of my skin, hot and insistent, leaving me cold.

My heartbeat pounded against my eardrums as the second hand on the wall clock ticked impossibly loud in my ears. Beside me, I could feel the steady rise and fall of breathing. The creak of bedsprings groaned as *they* shifted in bed, and I shut my eyes tight, willing this moment to end. Willing myself to wake up. Willing that this was all some false start. Willing myself to still be dreaming. Wishing that I hadn't opened my eyes at all.

Instead, the weight of a hand landed on my arm, and a sudden rush of pain dug into my flesh as unseen fingers clamped down like a vice.

My eyes flew open, and I swallowed a roar of pain, throwing myself from the bed. I tumbled to the floor, landing on all fours, and spun like a cornered dog to face an empty room. There was no one there. No one in the bed. No one in the room. Just me. The only sound, the ticking of the wall clock and my own labored breathing.

A throb of pain pulsed through my arm. I rolled up my shirt sleeve, tenderly examining the flesh from wrist to elbow. There, blooming like a flower, was the reddish, purpling imprint of a hand. The shadow of five fingers wrapped themselves around my forearm, long and thick. A phantom hand that dwarfed my own. This hadn't been a dream. This couldn't have been some sleeping, self-inflicted bruise. The proof was there on my flesh.

Sunlight continued to spill through the gauzy linen curtains hanging in the window; brighter than when I'd shut my eyes, but the light was devoid of all warmth. The room was cold. Empty. Still. My eyes darted around the room, searching for any sign of activity. Nothing moved. Keeping the wall at my back, I edged toward the door. Blindly, I grasped for the doorknob. With a twist, the door gave way behind me, and I stumbled from the room.

The rest of the apartment was as quiet and empty as when I got there; otherwise, I might as well have walked into a completely different home. That of a deranged person. The dining room chairs hung in the air, impossibly balanced atop one another. The four of them somehow leaned against one another with their legs jutting out at strange angles. They formed a towering, sculptural diamond of chairs in the center of the dining room. A bout of frantic laughter burst through the stillness of the apartment. It was my own. The realization was surprise enough to make me laugh even more, though nothing about the situation was funny. I turned, surveying the rest of the apartment.

When Kenny left, he took his couch with him, leaving the living room empty. So Bryan and I had made it a point to tastefully rearrange the remaining armchairs to fill the absence as best we could. Now, the armchairs were piled together in a mound. Their pillows and cushions each stacked atop one another to form a neat peak. A mini Everest in the center of the apartment. The various tall, skinny standing lamps that lived in different corners of the apartment were leaning against each other, a codependent cone of poles and light bulbs, balancing like the skeleton of a teepee. It was as if I could feel the screws of my sanity loosening, bit by bit.

That guy has a screw loose. A loose screw. Nuts. Bonkers. Bananas. The various colloquialisms for crazy spun through my head. These phrases floated along in common use, familiar as anything, but I'd never considered what they really meant. How they came to be. How does a person get to have a screw loose? Having suddenly found myself amid the process, I realized I didn't really want to know the answer. There was the laughter again. Bubbling up from my lips. Echoing through the apartment.

I needed something. Air. Water. Something natural. Something sure. Walking down the long hall toward the kitchen, I forced myself not to run, to maintain a normal, casual pace. I stretched my arm out to open the cabinet. I hated how my hand trembled as I swung it open. I willed my fingers to quit their twitching as I reached out to turn the knob on the sink. Water *whooshed* from the faucet, making a sound so normal, so everyday, so not-crazy, I almost wanted to cry. I filled the glass I'd retrieved from the cabinet and gulped it down, letting the faucet run. Letting the sound fill the kitchen with its mundane, miniature roar. The littlest waterfall powering the generator of my sanity.

I inhaled deeply and let the water flow. Gradually, my pulse seemed to normalize. In the back of the apartment, farthest from the windows' eastern exposure near the front, the kitchen was dimmer than the living and dining rooms. Yet, the white cabinets and tiles of the floor reflected the little sunlight that managed to seep into the kitchen. Generally, during the day, the sunshine streaming through the windows at the front of the apartment, along with the light that shone through the kitchen's one rear-facing window, was enough to illuminate the room without needing to turn on the overhead light.

Sitting there on the windowsill, basking in a small square of sun, was Bryan's relatively small collection of houseplants. A couple of ferns or something. Maybe basil? I don't know plants. All I knew was that, with Bryan's care and attention, they had always maintained their healthy green leafiness. Only now, they were all dead. Not just dead, corrupted. All the plants oozed there in their pots. Mushy, dark brown. Rotten. A musty smell, like mold and slime and decay, wafted to me from across the kitchen. It made me want to vomit.

I had to leave the apartment. As quickly as possible, I shut off the water. I raced to grab my keys and coat and ran down the stairs, swinging doors shut behind me as I went. I couldn't bring myself to look back as I left the place. I jammed the key in the lock, twisting it briskly, despite the grinding metal resistance of the aging mechanism, and walked away, beginning to lose the fight against running. As I jogged down the street, I choked down a manic laugh I couldn't bear to hear.

Chapter Ten

I welcomed the chill air on my face. The warmth of the sun attempted to burn through the morning's overcast of clouds as the day stretched closer and closer to noon. The farther I got from my apartment, the more everything that had happened there seemed less real. The events at the Sentinel Club seemed more like a dream than anything. Hazy. Insane. The whole morning, just a sequence of awful dreams. The hours since I'd opened the Rosebriar might as well have been years. But the tremor in my hands wasn't as ready to move on as my rationalizing mind seemed to be. The hollow feeling in my gut refused to embrace the numbing distance that a few hours' time had to offer, no matter how desperately I longed to do so myself.

Rust-colored leaves crunched under my shoes with each step as I walked aimlessly. The frosty fall breeze numbed my skin where it was exposed, but I hardly noticed. Instinctually, I made my way toward the boulevard. Long stretches of grass and trees flanked the busy roads leading to the roundabout in the center of Logan Square. Instead of heading west along Logan Boulevard in the direction of the roundabout's central column with its eagle and benches, I walked east. I had no real destination in mind. I just needed to walk.

After a while, I made my way over from Logan Square into Bucktown. Crossing over any one of Chicago's arbitrary borders between neighborhoods was always strange. Historically, the differences between them tended to relate to the heritage of their population. In a city like Chicago, where racism and segregation played such a huge part in the city's development, it was hard to move through the different areas without thinking about the city's history. Layers and layers of history. Overlapping. Forgotten.

As Logan Square itself became increasingly gentrified, the new, young, affluent, and predominately white occupants were hardly even aware of the neighborhoods' traditionally Latino residents being pushed out of their homes by rising property taxes. Most of the current occupants of Bucktown don't even know their neighborhood's name came from the Polish immigrants who first lived in the area, raising their goats, males of which are called bucks. These thoughts flitted through my mind as I walked past the rows of houses. Some perfect examples of old-school-Chicago architecture. With their weathered stone faces, these old buildings are testaments to Chicago's history, forgotten and otherwise.

Eventually, I found my way to Holstein Park. For a Monday morning, it was packed with people. Across the expanse of barren trees and dry grass, the looming brick school-like building of the field house swarmed with activity. The Chicago Park District had paired with area schools to host some sort of bullshit apple-pie festival, encouraging families who could afford to miss an afternoon of work to gather and celebrate the fall.

I worked my way through an onslaught of happy couples and smiling families. The scent of cinnamon and apples filled the air. Laughter and joyful conversation rose up from the middle of the park, and people were in little clumps all around me. Groups of friends, lovers, and families were everywhere. No one I recognized. Strangers all around. I made my way through the crowd, cutting through the various matching sets of smiles like a stone sinking to the bottom of a koi pond, all the while resisting a sudden urge to cry. In the distance, the Catholic Church of Saint Hedwig's green-copper dome rose above the other buildings and trees. Without thinking about it, I made my way in that direction.

The church sat there waiting, four blocks from the park with all its vibrancy and happy couples. Being in the apple-pie festival, surrounded by the warm bodies of all the people sipping cider, had made me feel miles away from the rest of humanity. I felt stained. The hand-shaped bruise on my arm, hidden under my sleeve, might as well have been a brand, setting me apart from all these other festival goers. Unseen, the bruise was like an invisible beacon, marking me as touched by some darkness I didn't understand.

I walked faster until I mounted the stone steps of Saint Hedwig's and was finally able to unclench the fists I'd pinned at my sides. My fingers were stiff, and my palms were marked with little half-moons from where my fingernails had sunk into the flesh of my hands. The roof, domed like a Roman shield, had marble statues of saints lining the perimeter of it like sentinels. There's nothing like fear to bring a lapsed Catholic running back to the Church. After everything that had occurred today, it seemed appropriate to find myself here even if I couldn't readily remember when I'd been to mass last.

Pulling the heavy oak door open, I submerged myself in the warm shadows of the candlelit interior. At the threshold of the sanctuary, I dipped my fingers into the room-temperature germy pool of holy water and dutifully made the sign of the cross, mumbling the names of God in triplicate as I did. Each step I took echoed in the cavernous hollow of the church. The place was empty. The dim quiet was comforting. Familiar. I'd never been inside Saint Hedwig's, yet, as I found a spot to kneel in the pew closest to the entrance, it occurred to me that after seeing one Catholic church, you've practically seen them all. There's a pious familiarity to them. It's surprising how comforting an idea that can be.

I clasped my hands together, interlaced my fingers, and closed my eyes. Effortlessly, the words to prayers I'd memorized as a child floated from my lips. I thought of my parents who had taught me these prayers. Prayers I still turned to in times like these. Times of need. Of hope. Of desperation.

Lapsed or not, like so many a millennial Mexican American, I couldn't entirely resist the pull of Catholicism. It wasn't a sense of devotion or loyalty to dogma, per se. The Roman Catholic Church had long ago decided people like me were going to hell. Yet, I still found myself here. Now. Drawn by a need for...what? Refuge? Comfort? Whether I was willing to admit it or not, the moment I entered the church I experienced exactly that. A sense of comfort. I had tapped into a cultural mode, rooted in my upbringing and beyond, echoing back through my family for generations. For as long as I could remember, when our family was in crisis, we turned to the Church. To prayer. To God.

History lessons about conquistadors and colonization had complicated my views of religion, almost as much as being a gay man had. If not more. Not far from where I knelt, a shrine bearing a statue of Saint Hedwig was nestled in a shadowy cloister. It was illuminated by flickering candlelight and the shards of jewel-toned sunlight that shone through any of the numerous stained-glass windows. A nearby plaque identified her as the patron of some sect of Polish priests. How fitting. She was a saint I knew little about. Not like La Virgen de Guadalupe, the iconic Mexican incarnation of the Virgin Mary, or even Saint Jude Thaddeus, the patron saint of impossible causes. Those were the saintly figures that mattered to me and my people, the ones I still found myself praying to. Lighting candles for. Just as my ancestors before me had folded their indigenous deities into the figures and mythology of Catholic saints, I'd maintained the beliefs that nurtured my soul, and let the rest roll off my back.

Over the years, I wrestled with guilt and self-hate, as have many survivors of a Catholic upbringing. The older I got, the more questions I asked; and the more I knew myself, I found organized religion to be nothing but a distillation of western civilization's colonial, patriarchal bullshit. Yet here I knelt. I needed something. Would I find it here?

From her cloister, Saint Hedwig glowered, judgmental and condescending. Tucked into the pews were missals, leather-bound texts stuffed with various readings from the Bible and outlines of the Catholic mass, presented for churchgoers to follow along. Books of hymns waited beside each copy. There weren't any Bibles. Just those truncated guidebooks to old rituals and curated excerpts from an infallible text, created by highly fallible men.

I forced myself to focus and, on my knees, I spoke the words of the Lord's Prayer, over and over again. The Our Fathers tumbled from my mouth in a loop, always ending with the same phrase: "deliver us from evil."

Yes, the Church had failed me in numerous ways. The Church had turned its back on me and the ones I loved. It was comprised of a congregation that loved to mutter snide "Hate the sin, love the sinner" sentiments while reassuring one another people like me were sure to face eternal damnation. For what? For being exactly how God made us. How often had I sat there in communion with people who could so blithely condemn others to an eternity of hellfire while turning a blind eye to their own hypocrisies? If these righteous, good people thought I deserved to burn for eternity, it must be so? Right? How could I ever undo the damage I'd done to myself by internalizing these so-called morals? But though the Church had failed me, I wasn't convinced that meant God had. I let my fingers lightly touch the bruises on my upper arm. The fear that had gripped me all morning long softened.

Across the expansive chamber of the church, on the opposite side of the shrine to Saint Hedwig, were other shrines. The shadowy alcove housing statues of the Virgin Mary flickered with candlelight, and the scent of aging floral arrangements hung on the air.

An image floated into my mind: my sister. The train of her white dress trailing behind her as she presented roses to a statue of La Virgen de Guadalupe on the day of her wedding. I remembered a swell of love for her in that moment as well as a pang of longing, knowing that I could never have a wedding like hers in a place like this. It had been a beautiful wedding. Kenny had been my date. He'd met scores of my extended family that night. He'd been in the photos. I'd imagined what such festivities would look like when we eventually got married.

Standing, I made my way over to this Mary's alcove. I reached into my wallet and pulled out a wrinkled dollar bill. After stuffing it into the wooden collection box in front of a bank of prayer candles at Mary's feet, I knelt again. This time, on the single kneeling bench stationed before the Holy Mother and her candles. I lit one, reciting a Hail Mary.

Years ago, at a Christmas service I'd attended with my parents and sister, I had prayed to be less lonely. I had prayed to find someone to love me: someone that I could love. It was Christmas, and I'd been considering presents and wish lists; it seemed as good a prayer as any. Kenny and I had met the following March. I remember thinking how my prayers had been answered.

Stupid. I was stupid. An idiot. When I found out he had cheated on me, I prayed again. I prayed for an end to the pain I'd found myself in, for freedom from the inescapable sense that I was worthless and pathetic. Unworthy of love. He was the only man I had ever loved, and I was left broken. Here I was, praying again. The bruise on my arm throbbed.

Part of me knew I wasn't unloved. I had my family. I had longed to reach out to them over the course of the past couple of weeks. I'd wanted to call my mother countless time. I wanted to text my sister. But something stopped me. I looked down at the bandages on my wrists. I knew how much what I'd done would hurt them. I was ashamed. Embarrassed. My mother had raised me to be stronger than that. My sister would scoff at the thought of me hanging my worth on the love of some guy. My father would *tsk* at seeing me so utterly broken by something so mundane as a man's infidelity.

They loved me, and all they wanted for me was to be happy. And that was one thing that I had utterly failed them at. How could I face them? How could I put them through the pain of seeing me brought so low? I couldn't. I wouldn't. They could never know.

With its arching ceilings, the vast interiority of Saint Hedwig's made me feel small. Each breath, each footprint, each sigh echoed, magnifying as the sound reverberated off the gilded stone walls. Rows and rows of hardwood pews all faced the altar on a raised dais at the far end of the chamber. From past the massive bronze crucifix that hung beyond the altar, a door opened and closed. The sound thundered throughout the otherwise quiet church. No longer alone, I froze, vulnerable.

Saint Hedwig's was beautiful; yet, with the silence shattered, everything shifted. The shadows seemed longer. Darker. The flickering candlelight became weak and stuttering against the darkness. The faces of the saints transformed, becoming severe and sinister; watching, silent and accusatory, with eyes that followed your every move.

With the door slam, someone had entered the sanctuary. In an instant, I was ill at ease. The sound of footsteps on stone, rhythmic and paced, tumbled out from the shadows. They seemed to be coming from everywhere and nowhere at all. Logically, I could place the source of the footsteps as coming from behind the altar; yet in my heart, they were bats with black, leathery wings, flocking everywhere in a dark cloud surrounding me.

From around the dais, a priest started to make his way down the aisle, aimless at first, and then I sensed him notice me. He paused. Almost imperceptibly, he started to turn my way. With a quick sign of the cross, I finished my prayers and rose from my knees. I glanced once more at the statue of the Virgin Mary. She looked scared. I hadn't noticed before. Then, a voice as soft as a sigh and as gentle as an exhale, floated to me from I don't know where. "Run."

The shadows around the priest seemed to have thickened somehow. Perhaps it was a cloud bank passing overhead, momentarily overshadowing the stained-glass windows. Regardless, in the dim light, the priest's pale skin almost glowed. A shock of his blond hair flew into disarray as his head shook in all directions. He seized jerkily and twitched before freezing, contorted: still as stone. Motionless as the statue of Saint Hedwig. He was facing me, still halfway across the church. That's when I heard him laughing. A low, wheezing, animal-like sound. I shot a final glance at the anguished face of Jesus, an eternal grimace of pain as he hung from the cross high above the altar, and I ran.

As rapidly as I could without breaking into a run, I headed for the front door. At first, I couldn't tell if the sound of footsteps bouncing off the walls of the church were my own feet slapping against the stone floor or those of the priest. Then, I became aware of a distinct rhythm. While I had resisted the urge to run, the priest had broken into a sprint. He was approaching fast in the darkness. The sound of his laugh and labored breathing reverberated. As I fled past the pews toward the exit, that laugh chased me. It was all-encompassing. It sounded so near as though he was breathing down the back of my neck. I didn't turn around to see how much he had closed the distance. I abandoned the quick walk for a full-on sprint, and I didn't look back. I just ran.

Chapter Eleven

I burst through the doors of Saint Hedwig's, staggering down the stairs. With a crash, the heavy doors slammed shut behind me. The sound was enough to cause me to jump, and I used the jolt to resist stalling, to keep moving even if I was at a loss for where to go. On autopilot, one foot in front of the other, I let muscle memory put as much distance as possible between me and the church. On instinct, I found myself headed back toward Holstein Park. Back toward the apple-pie fest. It was my only option. I tried my best to keep my face a neutral mask. Better to appear cold and distant than fractured. Manic.

Fighting the urge to run, I found myself speed walking, resisting the need to look behind me. More a reflex than anything else, I pulled out my phone. My thumb started to type K, E, and N into the dialing screen. Before I had deleted Kenny's number from my phone, the K alone would have brought up his number. As it was, there was nothing. My phone had no suggestions for me.

I hadn't entirely blocked Kenny from my digital sphere. Not yet. Unfriended, yes. Unfollowed, sure. But the idea of clicking that block button was somehow something I couldn't bring myself to do. So, given that no one memorizes phone numbers anymore, by deleting his from my cell, I couldn't call him even if I wanted to. And I did. But to the furthest extent of my phone's knowledge, Kenny did not exist. If only my thumb were on the same page. If only every part of me were. If only Kenny did not exist. If only I didn't.

Without realizing it, I came to a halt. Around me, crowds were milling. Surrounded by festival goers enjoying themselves, I stood frozen, unable to peel my eyes from my phone. It sat there, confused as to which K, E, N–named stranger I might be trying to contact. I could do nothing but stand there and stare at it, only to be confounded when it sprung to life in my hand.

Still on silent mode, the phone didn't ring but rather vibrated, glowing as the screen lit up with the face of Maisey. The ID picture I assigned her in my phone was a selfie we took together years ago in college. Waves of relief pulsed through my body as the vibrations of the silenced phone's ringing spread up my arm. With a swipe of my finger, I answered the call. "Maise, thank God."

"Hey! I heard about what happened at the Rosebriar. Are you okay?" The sound of my friend's voice coming through the phone seemed to unlock something inside me. Streams of hot tears coursed down my face.

"No. I'm really not."

"Where are you? Gabe? Gabe? Answer me." Her directness cut through my tear-fogged vision. Increasingly self-conscious amid the crowd, I wiped my runny nose on the back of my hand with a sniffle. I swiped at my cheeks with affected casualness and wished I could turn invisible.

"Um, I'm at this apple-pie festival thing in Bucktown."

"Are you in Holstein Park?"

"Yeah. Near the field house."

"Just head to the playground. I'll be there soon."

"Maisey, you don't have to do that," I said, though I desperately wanted to see her. In that moment, I wanted nothing more than to let Maisey take me into one of her hugs. I needed it. A moment of human kindness.

"Meet me on the playground. Swings. I'll be there in fifteen." She hung up.

Lowering the phone from my ear, I made my way through the crowd. The playground was on the other side of the field house, so I headed in that direction. Following the stream of human traffic, I darted inside and made my way to the bathroom. Thankfully, it was empty. With high ceilings and massive windows, light filled the restroom, bouncing off of the white tiles and long mirror that stretched across the wall above a row of sinks. The length of the wall opposite was split, half urinals and half stalls. Crossing to a sink, I turned on the faucet and let the hot water fill my cupped hands. I splashed it across my face and looked into the mirror. I looked like shit. Then, out of the corner of my eye, I caught a flash of movement. Or did I?

In the periphery of my vision, I thought I'd seen something. In the mirror, the door to one of the stalls seemed to swing, ever so slightly. Without hesitation, I left the bathroom. I walked through the people lingering in the halls and made my way back out of the field house and around to the playground.

I took a deep breath. Tension had wound up all the tendons in my body, tight as the strings on a violin. With a shake, I made an effort to loosen up my limbs. The festival stands and banners on the northside of the field house had drawn most of the crowd away from the park on the southern side, and as such, there were no children on the playground.

Wind moved the swings hanging from the heavy metal beams of the swing set. Back and forth. Three pendulums. A number of golden leaves danced down the slide. Grabbing the chains of the center swing, I steadied the seat beneath myself and sat down. My feet dangled off the ground, and the chill fall air had made the chains a dull aching cold in my bare hands. I hung there, swinging in the wind. Above me, the expanse of the gray sky stretched on forever.

Breathing in the cool air for the slightest of moments, I felt like a ghost of myself. For the briefest moment, I was the me from before. Before the events of the morning. Sure, I was once again a broken, damaged, and unbearably sad version of myself, but a version at least grounded in some unarticulated sense of reality. Sitting there on that swing, I remembered a time, only hours ago, when I wasn't questioning my own sanity. I had once stood on solid ground. But things change. Quickly. Hell, I was once loved and strong and whole. And now that those things had just been tossed out the window, maybe it was only right for my mind to follow suit. There had to be a rational explanation for the things I'd seen, experienced. Right?

I continued to swing back and forth on the empty playground. The sharp chill of the wind made my lips tingle in a familiar way. The same way they had when Kenny and I had shared our first kiss.

We'd met in the cold of Chicago's early spring. It was March, and winter still held its grip over the city. We'd met for drinks and talked for hours, and when Kenny offered to walk me home, I tried to decline. It was too cold. I lived nearby. It wasn't far enough for it to be a thing. But he insisted.

As we made our way through the frosty street, he intertwined his gloved fingers with mine, and together our hands swung back and forth: one fist, a pendulum swaying between the two of us back and forth. Sitting on that swing, I did the same. I swung back and forth as I sank into the muck of my memories. My face had started to tingle with the bite of the wind just as it did now; but here, instead of Kenny pulling me to him, closing the distance between our lips, and warming mine with his, my lips grew cold. I continued to swing. It sucked how every little thing made me think about him. I couldn't even be cold without it reminding me of my ex. Being cold is shitty enough as it is. The fact that it made me sad is just overkill.

I looked at the park around me. Even the run-of-the-mill playground equipment brought aching sense memories of Kenny and our relationship to the forefront of my mind. It was in a park very similar to this one that we said "I love you" for the first time.

Weeks after that March evening when we'd shared our first, frost-sparked kiss, we went dancing. Kenny hated dancing. He wasn't particularly good at it, and his insecurity gave him an adorable boyishness I found endearing, so when he asked to call it a night early, I agreed. We stumbled our way onto the 'L' and back toward his place.

Beyond his backyard, there was a small neighborhood park with a modest playground and swing set. Tipsy and enamored, we made our way into the park that lay there, empty and shining in the moonlight. Our feet crunched on the wood chips. I pulled him into an embrace, throwing our tenuous balance off-kilter and landing us in a heap on the sharp incline of the slide. I didn't even feel the words as they tumbled from my lips. "I love you." When he repeated the words to me, the moonlight turned the world to silver around us. Or maybe it was the booze that made it seem so. Or the haze of my memory. Or love. Either way, that park was not this one. I shivered as a gust of wind cut through my coat.

"Gabe!" Pushing a large expensive-looking stroller, Maisey made her way from the edge of the park toward the playground. Even from where I sat on the swing, I could see the concern on her face. I could almost read her mind. *Is it happening again?* Nervous all of a sudden, I tugged the cuff of my sleeve down over the cotton bandages on my wrists.

"Maisey." As she came nearer, I could see she had thoroughly bundled up Shaun against the cold. She might as well have been pushing around a child-sized bundle of coats and blankets in the stroller. I could barely see the toddler beneath all the layers she'd wrapped him in.

Maisey had been Shaun's nanny literally since he was born. His young well-to-do parents hired her a week or so before he'd been due. Now that Shaun was two and a half years old, Maisey was allowed to take him out of the house. Within reason. The fact that the McNeals lived in Bucktown made the occasional excursion to the playground at Holstein Park reasonable enough.

Finally, she was within arm's reach. I jumped from the swing and pulled her into a hug, swallowing any sobs that threatened to launch me into a fresh bout of tears. She wrapped her arms around me tightly, hugging me back.

Maisey and I met in undergrad, eventually becoming roommates and best friends. She was a staggeringly beautiful person on a regular day. Everyone said so. The number of straight men who'd approach her on a regular basis was proof enough. The number of straight men who approached me when we'd be out together and she'd step away momentarily, eager to ask what her deal was or to commiserate in appreciation of her beauty, was exhaustive. But seeing her here, when I so desperately needed her to be, made me really see how beautiful she was. Had I never noticed before? The straight, silken, chestnut-brown hair, the ice-blue eyes, straight white teeth, the Rory Gilmore complexion; none of that meant anything.

The strength of her arms wrapped around me as my tears soaked into her scarf was enough to keep me from falling utterly apart, and in her work-mess baby-stained nanny sweatpants and clashing layered coat/scarf/hat combo, she had never looked so beautiful to me. She'd seen me cry before. She'd seen me puke before. She'd seen me at my best and she sure as hell had seen me at my worst. She visited me in the hospital afterward. And here she was now. "I'm so glad to see you."

"Of course," she said, her voice muffled by my shoulder. "Now, tell me everything."

I started from the beginning with that morning and my running late on the train like an asshole. Tardy on my first day back from leave. I told her about Leslie, about my conversations with the back-of-house staff, about Rod. The man. The call. What happened at my apartment. At the church. Hearing the words spilling out of my mouth like bile made me feel almost sick. Or rather, it made me feel like I had just been sick. That I had just puked up something vile that had been festering inside me. Seeing it in a puddle at my feet, hearing it spoken out loud made me feel embarrassed, exhausted, and gross. But also, better. Somehow cleaner on the inside. I looked at Maisey, afraid to see my own fear echoed on her face: that I was crazy.

Maisey's lips were pursed in concentration. There was no judgment, though traces of concern drew her eyebrows together. Her face was the epitome of a sight for sore eyes. The wind tousled the strands of brown hair that framed her face, having slipped out from beneath the winter hat topped with a little pom-pom that she wore. Her blue eyes looked at me with a self-assured stillness that I'd always admired. She gently pushed the stroller back and forth. Shaun dozed beneath the layers where she'd tucked him away.

With a shiver, she looked at me and said, "Let's go."

"Where?"

"Somewhere warm. Somewhere with food and drink. Somewhere we can think about what all this means."

I followed my friend out of the park.

Chapter Twelve

"I'm not saying that it's all in your head—"

"But—"

"—but I have to ask, how much of all this *might* be in your head?" Bouncing Shaun on her knee, Maisey looked across the table at me. It wasn't an irrational question, and she somehow managed to present it without any judgment in her voice.

"I—I don't know."

"I mean, yes, you were attacked. That is a fact. There's security video footage. News coverage, blah blah blah. Dude is in a coma. Fact."

"Right."

"But the phone call? I mean, you'd just gone through a traumatic event." As she spoke, she held up an additional finger with each point. "You woke up early, so...tired, right? And let's be honest, you haven't been in the best...place, mentally, emotionally...recently, right?" Her eyes glanced toward my wrist.

Part of me appreciated Maisey's directness. The fact that no matter what, she wouldn't treat me any different. Still, part of me would have appreciated just a little less directness from her in this particular case.

Now self-conscious, I tugged down the sleeves of my shirt. "I know."

"I'm only saying this so we can think about this rationally."

"Please! Yes. That is exactly what I need. Reason! Rationality! Fuck...I feel like I'm losing it." My hands tingled anxiously. I cracked my knuckles before starting to tap out a subconscious SOS in Morse code on the tabletop.

"Could you stop that please?"

"Stop what?"

Maisey raised a single eyebrow aimed at my twitching hands.

"Sorry." I proceeded to silently tear apart the paper napkin I'd been given with my coffee.

With a deep breath, Maisey took my hands in her free one while the other stabilized the squirming toddler on her lap. "You are not losing it. Even when...even when things were bad, you hadn't 'lost it.' That's not what I'm saying. You were in pain, okay? What I *am* saying is after the morning you've had, you're on the train, you get a rand-o call from a telemarketer and...and things get misconstrued. You remember things differently than they might have happened. It's a possibility at least, yeah?"

"Maybe? Now I wish I hadn't deleted it. But at the time...I dunno. No. You're right, you're right. I hear you, but"—as discreetly as possible, I pulled my arm out of my coat and pulled up my shirt sleeve to show her my hand-marked forearm—"what about this?"

Tenderly, she reached out her fingers to trace the hand-shaped bruise. "Damn, dude. Does it hurt?"

I flinched instinctively before she could check, pulling my sleeve down and shouldering my jacket back on. "Yeah."

"Well—"

"And no, I didn't do it myself."

"Well," she began again, pointedly, "it might be psychosomatic."

"What?"

"Haven't you ever read about those women who want to be pregnant so bad, their body actually starts to change, like, as though they *were* pregnant? People's brains can actually cause their bodies to react to stimuli that doesn't really exist."

"Where are you getting all this?"

"Shaun and I watch a lot of daytime television, don't we, Shaun?" Shaun responded with a giggle as Maisey hefted him back into his stroller.

"So...you're saying...that you *do* think I did this to myself."

"No! Well, yes. Kind of. I mean, A, *might* have. And B, not on purpose or even consciously."

"And the shit that happened in my apartment? The priest?" I could feel myself applying Maisey's suggested lens of reason to the things that had happened so far today.

"Sleepwalking? Or Bryan playing some fucked-up joke? Your landlord rearranging furniture? The priest thing could have been a misunderstanding?" It was as though she had a list of logical explanations for all the illogical things I'd experienced that morning. "Maybe the priest thought you were, I dunno, some hoodlum he—he—he had to chase out of the church before you stole some silver candlesticks...or something."

"I'm not Jean Valjean."

"I'm just saying that if you want... there can be a rational explanation for everything that has happened to you today."

"If I want?"

"If you don't..." She paused. A frown of determination had settled across her face. "You consider the alternative." Something about the way she said that rang a bell in my mind. I could practically feel the vibrations ripple down my spine.

"The alternative."

"Stop repeating everything I say." She let out an exasperated sigh and again took my hands in hers. "I don't think you're crazy, Gabe. I don't. And you can look at everything you've just told me and try to squeeze it all into the neat little boxes of reasonable explanations and logic, but why? If you're not crazy, and if the things that have happened to you today *don't* have reasonable explanations, then maybe we should take into consideration the *unreasonable* ones." Maisey looked around the cafe.

Shaun had started to doze in the coziness of his stroller. Behind the cash register, the teenage barista scrolled on her phone through what I could only assume was some stupid social media feed or another. Across the coffee shop, an older woman sat, reading a paperback novel. No one was paying us any attention.

Maisey took her time before starting to talk again. It was almost as though she had to reckon with something inside herself before she could start. It was like she was weighing whether to tell me something or not. I wasn't entirely sure I wanted to hear what she had to tell.

"When I was little, we used to go visit my grandma in Oklahoma. Every summer. She lived in this teeny little town, and her house was out in the middle of nowhere. Don't get me wrong, I loved my meemaw and everything, but I used to *hate* going on those visits."

"Why?"

"There was something in that house." Maisey generally had a fair complexion, yet now, her usual healthy, if pale skin, had gone even more pallid. "I knew it. Even as a child. You could feel it when you were there. This sense of...being watched? You could be the only person in the whole damn house, but you were never alone. Do you know what I mean?"

"I do." My voice sounded like a shallow whisper as her words rolled around in my head like a marble, shifting as it made loops in my mind. *Damn house. Damn house. Damn house. Damned house. Damned. House. Damned.*

"I remember one time. My grandma and my mom went...I dunno, to the store or something. They said they'd be right back, so they left me alone. Meemaw had this tire swing out front, so I figured fine, you know? I'd just play outside on the swing until they got back. But then, of course—"

"You had to go to the bathroom." I couldn't help but smile, even through the subtle sense of unease that had been building since Maisey started her story. She was my best friend, and I knew her intimately, and one thing I definitely knew about Maisey, the girl had a bladder the size of a pea.

In my head I imagined her, a small girl in pigtails and overalls, standing in the Oklahoma heat, looking at the emptiness of her grandma's house from the yard. Doing an impatient dance, weighing her options.

"I had to pee! I had to. I was, what? Maybe eight or so? Too old to have an accident, you know? I couldn't just piss myself. So...I went in the house. I ran to the bathroom. Went as fast as I could, like, didn't even wash my hands. Didn't flush. Just went in, took care of business, and tried to get the fuck out of there..." She faltered. She took a deep breath. I could see this was hard for her.

"Maisey, you don't have to—"

"No. No. It's fine. It's just...I still remember. You know? God. I can still feel it, like on my skin." There were tears in her eyes. "The sweat on my skin, like, it was hot. Summer in Oklahoma hot. But when I stepped out from the bathroom, the sweat, it all, like, evaporated. Like, instantly. And I heard this, this sound. It was crying. The sound of a child crying. And, I mean, at the time, I was a child too, you know? I was a kid, but I remember hearing this kid crying and something about it was just so...so...sad.

"And... I, uhm, I turned to run down the hall, to get the fuck out of there, you know, to run back outside to the swing, but when I turned...there was this woman. Standing there. I had never seen her before. Never in my life. But she was wearing these old-timey clothes, and her back was facing me. She was looking off toward the sound of the crying, and I just got this, this...this sense that this was a bad lady. Bad. Like, capital B. Bad. I felt it.

"And, I was frozen. I couldn't move or think or breathe or...or...I just...I was so scared, Gabe. I was. So. Scared. And she started to turn my way. So slowly. Like impossibly slowly. She started to turn toward me...and, like, at that very moment, I heard my mom's car rolling up on the gravel of Meemaw's driveway, and I was able to move again."

I didn't realize I had been holding my breath.

With a short bark of a laugh, Maisey wiped away the tear that had subtly started to roll down her cheek. "I threw a *fit*." She laughed again. "You know me. I can be a real brat sometimes. Well, I refused to go back into that house. We ended up cutting that visit to Meemaw short." I had to laugh too. Then Maisey got a little quiet. "I don't think I ever told that story to anyone before."

"Well, what happened?"

"Nothing. Meemaw moved a couple years after that. Apparently, the town made the house a historical landmark. It used to belong to the headmistress of one of the Indian schools way back when. You know, the Indian Residential Schools—?"

"You've gotta be shitting me." I had read about the abuse Native American kids had endured at the American Indian Boarding Schools during the turn of the century. It was horrific.

"Hand to God." The color had returned to Maisey's face. She cleared her throat with a small cough and took a sip from her coffee. Maisey looked over at the sleeping Shaun thoughtfully before returning her sharp blue eyes to me. "I believe you, Gabe. I don't think you're crazy." I wonder if Maisey could ever know just how much that meant.

"Thank you."

"So now, looking at the facts of the situation..."

"Right. I just, I don't even know what the situation is."

"Well, it seems to me, and I'm no expert here, but it seems to me that something, ugh, what? Supernatural?" A small, almost bitter laugh slipped from Maisey's mouth like a cough. "Something supernatural is going on. *Something* seems to have...fixated on you."

"Awesome."

"Your sarcasm, apparently, doesn't balk in the face of fear."

"Well, thank God for that 'cause every other part of me is balked the fuck out."

With a wry smile, Maisey took another sip of her coffee. She looked at me, and with the slightest arch of her eyebrow, she said, "So, now the question becomes, what are you gonna do about it?"

Chapter Thirteen

The warmth of the coffee shop and the heat of my espresso (or maybe just the caffeine) had finally thawed out the stiffness in my joints. The thick scent of coffee grounds and reheated pastries filled the air. "Maisey, I..."

"Shut up." After standing from her seat across from me, my friend pulled me into a hug. "Save the thank-yous for later, kay?" Glancing down at the still snoozing Shaun, she continued, "I have to get this one back to his house. Are you gonna be okay?"

The thought of being alone again gave me pause. "Yeah. I'll be fine."

"Gabe, don't bullshit me."

"I dunno. Being alone sounds kind of awful right now..." Before I could finish, Maisey pulled out her phone and was typing away. "What are you doing?"

"What do you think?"

"Ordering a pizza."

"Shut up." Almost immediately, her phone dinged. "Bryan will be outside in five."

"Seriously?"

"What?"

"He's working."

"So?"

"So, it's kinda less than convenient, don't you think?" Though Bryan and I had been roommates for over two years, and we were definitely friends, the idea of imposing on him during his workday made me cringe. I hated the idea of being a burden. Maisey and I had the sort of well-worn friendship that made hitting her up out of the blue feel like much less of an inconvenience. "I mean, I don't need a babysitter."

"No. What you need is to get better at asking for what it is you *really* need. You don't want to be alone at the moment. Well, we got someone for you to hang out with. He said he was just about to take a break for lunch anyways. Easy peasy."

"Maise. He's working."

"Dude. He's an Uber driver. There's zero reason you can't ride shotgun for a while."

I couldn't think of a valid argument. "Thanks."

"*That* is a thank you I will allow." Shrugging on her coat and other winter gear, Maisey glanced over to double-check that Shaun was well bundled against the cold. "I'm gonna head out."

"'Kay." As Maisey pushed the stroller toward the door, I followed. She opened the door to the jingle from the small bell hanging over the threshold of the coffeeshop, then paused. I stepped around her and attempted to hold the door open so she could maneuver the clumsy expensive stroller out of the shop, but Maisey didn't move.

"Gabe...be careful. Okay? All of this...whatever is going on, I'm willing to bet things are gonna get worse before they get better."

"Story of my life." I tried to give her a smile. "Still waiting for the better part to come around. So, at this point, this is all just more of the same."

She smiled back, but the smile didn't reach her eyes. Here was one of my strongest friends, but just like when she was telling me the story of her grandmother's house, I could almost see her as a little girl. Young, vulnerable. Afraid. But here and now, she wasn't afraid for herself. She was afraid for me.

"I think...I know that you'll be okay, Gabe. I feel it in my gut. Yeah? But whatever it is that seems to be fixated on you, or whatever...it wants to hurt you. That much is clear. Don't let it. 'Kay?" In all our years as friends, I struggled to think of a time Maisey had spoken to me like this.

"Okay, Maise. I'll try." She looked at me, and I could see her willing the doubt from her gaze. The fierce blue of her eyes steeled with a determination that made me hungry for the same confidence Maisey had. Confidence in the idea that I would be okay. I wish I could feel that. "I'll try."

With a quick peck of a kiss on the cheek, Maisey pushed her dozing ward off into the chill gray of the afternoon. Following after her, I stepped out of the warmth of the coffee shop and stood there as my friend proceeded to turn the corner.

I sighed, and my breath turned into a cloud of fog in the air. I slipped my phone from my pocket and checked the time, half expecting a text from Bryan saying he'd picked up one last rider and was running late. A message saying Uber was on a rush period, and he'd have to see me later. *Sorry, dude. Don't have time for a ride-along right now.*

"Hop in, loser, we're going shopping." I looked up from my phone, startled. Leaning across the empty passenger seat, my roommate, Bryan, smiled at me through the rolled-down window closest to the curb. The shiny metallic-blue car gleamed with a recently washed freshness. I smiled at Bryan's *Mean Girls* reference and flung open the passenger door to climb into the warmth of the car's heated interior.

"Thanks, dude." Bryan pulled away from the curb, his eyes focused on oncoming traffic, reaching to switch off the radio without needing to look for the dial. "Are you sure it's cool for me to be riding along with you?"

"Come on, dude, it's Uber. I'm not a fucking limo driver. You eat?"

"Nah. Maisey and I just grabbed coffee. Not much of an appetite."

"I bet." He paused. He looked at me out of the corner of his eye. "You want to talk about it?"

"I..." I took a deep breath. Talking through things with Maisey had been like cleaning the gravel out from a scraped knee. It needed to be done, and I felt better now, but the rehashing of it all had been painful. The idea of going over that morning's events again so soon was not appealing in the least. "I don't think so."

"Cool cool." I looked out the window as we passed the numerous trees that lined the road, making our way back to the boulevard. Without taking my eyes from the rusted-orange leaves, I could feel Bryan relax behind the wheel. I wasn't sure what exactly Maisey had told him or how much he had gleaned about the Rosebriar incident from the news, or Facebook, or wherever, but he'd definitely gathered enough to be spooked. "Well, I'm hungry, so how's McDonald's sound, eh?"

Smiling despite myself, I reached out to turn the radio back on. Bryan's phone sat in a holster jutting out from the windshield. A blue dot traveled along the navigation app as we drove up Kedzie, back in the general direction of my apartment, before looping around the eagle-topped pillar in the center of the roundabout where Logan Boulevard and Milwaukee intersected.

I hated driving in the city. When I was younger, I was in no rush to get my driver's license. In fact, I waited until I was eighteen to even take driver's ed. I'd never owned a car. I guess I was never a big fan of driving in general, but Bryan seemed to enjoy it. Easily shifting lanes, he turned into the drive-thru lane of the McDonald's.

Across the street, the old-school marquee of the Logan movie theater rose to the sky. The whole interior of the movie theater had been rehabbed in a faux-art-deco style—an homage to the place's 1915 origins. They had a decent bar, fairly cheap concessions, and showed new releases at super affordable prices. I loved that place. Almost every Saturday, if neither of us had to work, Kenny and I would make the ten-minute walk over from our apartment to catch a matinee. I looked down at the anchor bound around my wrist. The thick cotton bandage underneath. "...anything?"

"Huh?" I looked over to Bryan. His face was a careful mask, devoid of judgment.

"I said, are you sure you don't want anything?" Behind him, the McDonald's drive-thru voice box hummed expectantly.

"Uh, yeah. I'm fine."

"I'm getting you nuggets," Bryan said, turning back to shout through his rolled-down window "Can you also add on an order of McNuggets please?" A muffled voice from outside of the car answered in the affirmative and instructed us to pull up to the next window.

"I said, I was fine."

"Yeah, but you were lying." He chuckled. The way he said it was so matter-of-fact it took me a moment to realize that he was right. I was hungry. I wasn't fine. I hadn't been fine for a while now. I wasn't fooling him, myself, or anyone else. And as we pulled up to the next window, I realized it didn't matter. I was decidedly not fine, and that was okay. For the moment at least.

Chapter Fourteen

It was shocking how fast Bryan ate his burger. One second it was there. The next it was gone. He made quick work of the fries too. It was cartoonish. I took my time with the chicken nuggets, careful not to spill barbecue sauce all over his car. It seems dumb, but the simple act of eating those chicken nuggets, the familiarity of it, was reassuring. It was comfort food. I couldn't count the times or places I'd had nuggets. In Happy Meals as a kid, in the cafeteria throughout middle and high school, in the dorms at Columbia downtown, and on days when I was hungry and had five dollars in my bank account—I could still get an order for a dollar. They were always there. They were always comforting. I took a breath and focused on appreciating the simple normalcy of sitting in a friend's car eating chicken nuggets. Considering the day that I'd had so far, I needed to feel normal. Even if normal is relative at best.

An Uber passenger sat in the back seat, tapped away on her phone quietly. When she had hopped in, Bryan confirmed that her name was Tasha. I'd almost forgotten she was there, but then the gentle sound of her acrylic nails tapping against the glass of her screen or the *whoosh* of notifications served as a reminder. She'd giggle or scoff in response to whatever she was reading, then more tapping. Beside her on the back seat sat a bubblegum-pink Lululemon yoga mat, rolled into a foam tube. Everything she had was branded and labeled. From her highlighter-pink Michael Kors purse to the glass bottle of Gwyneth Paltrow–endorsed Brew Dr. Kombucha she'd pulled from her Burberry tote bag. In a brief moment between messaging, she took a final sip from the Kombucha and returned it to the depths of her massive tote.

On the radio, Bryan had some random station playing music I was barely listening to. Softly, Sting and the Police underscored our drive. I hadn't realized just how creepy the lyrics to "Every Breath You Take" were. I twisted the radio dial until some inoffensive, old-timey music started to seep from the radio. The brassy sound of horns and a man's voice filled the car.

"Dude, what is this?"

I shrugged.

"Ted Lewis, 'I Ain't Got Nobody (And Nobody Cares For Me),' 1928," Tasha piped up from the back seat, eyes still glued to the screen of her phone.

"Ha-ha. Yeah? That's crazy! How'd you know that?" Bryan sounded legitimately impressed. "You listen to a lot of this kind of music?"

"Ew. No. Shazam. Obviously." She flashed her phone's screen our way. The song-identifying app had turned up a grainy black-and-white image of a guy in a suit, holding his top hat above him. Then, Tasha returned to her texting or whatever it was she was tapping away at. Ted Lewis's voice filled the car—*Had a sweetheart once I loved, and I was happy as could be; but now he's gone and left me here for someone else, you see. I ain't got nobody, and nobody cares for me. That's why I'm sad and lonely*—then click, and nothing. Without taking his eyes off the road, Bryan reached out a hand and turned off the radio. He did it casually. But for the briefest moment,

I caught him flick his eyes over to me in the passenger seat. I pretended not to notice.

Instead, I looked out the window at the city flying by. We were dropping Tasha off in River North, and since we picked her up back in Logan Square, the Uber's navigation system had instructed Bryan to take the 94 South. Buildings, the domes of churches, and the occasional park *whooshed* by as the Chicago skyline loomed in the distance, getting closer and closer.

Bryan took a sip from his massive soda. He jostled the ice around in his cup, never taking his eyes off the traffic in front of him. I could feel him wanting to say something, and I couldn't help but smile. He wanted to—*needed to—*diffuse the silence. It was just the way Bryan was. He never sat in silence for long. Every time I walked into the apartment and he was home alone, there was always music playing or the TV blaring in the background. He constantly wore headphones blasting music while he worked or walked.

He was typically the master of idle chitchat. At bars and cafes, he was the first to strike up a conversation with a stranger. When Tasha's ride first began, he'd tried to make conversation.

"River North, huh? Headed to work?"

"Sorry, I'm kinda in the middle of something?"

She hadn't even looked up from her phone. The hard line of her blonde bangs partially obscured her downcast eyes. The upward inflection of her rebuff put a quick end to Bryan's chitchat, and now, without the vintage nasality of Ted Lewis' voice, we were sitting in silence.

We moved closer and closer to downtown, closer and closer to the hotel. Closer to the Rosebriar Room. My eyes tracked the blue dot across the map of Bryan's Uber app.

My mind traced the shrinking distance between us and *that place*. I finished my nuggets and snapped the radio dial back on. No longer Ted Lewis or Sting. This time the radio blared some random Beyoncé song. Thank God.

"You okay?" Bryan asked quietly.

"Yeah. Yeah. It was just...getting too quiet in here."

"Hey, that's my line." Bryan's eyes flicked from me to the rearview mirror and then to the backseat. Tasha hadn't looked up from her phone again, though now she was mouthing the lyrics to "Love on Top," oblivious. Bryan rolled his eyes. I tried to stifle my laugh.

"Okay, getting close." Bryan got off the highway, taking Chicago Avenue toward the lake. After a few blocks, he turned down a side street and then another before eventually pulling up in front of a CorePower.

Once, I had taken a hot-yoga class with Maisey at a CorePower in Uptown. She had recently found herself able to afford a membership following a raise from the family she nannied for. I tagged along, able to get in as her guest. The class was fine, but when I asked the weirdly tan ponytailed dude behind the front desk about membership, he kindly let me know, "Memberships are kinda pricey, probs out of your price range. But we offer a discount to peeps who volunteer to clean up around the studio." I hadn't been back since.

"Thanks, Tasha."

Without a response, Tasha climbed out of the back seat. After the door slammed shut, Bryan looked over at me.

"Cute but horrible attitude."

He pulled the car out from the curb, heading south. Though the Sentinel Club was more than a few blocks away across the river, its presence was heavy in my mind.

Looming. The closer I got, the more I understood I was being pulled back there. Being drawn to it. Like water swirling down a drain. I was caught in its gravitational pull.

"Gabe? You okay? Looking a little pale."

"Fine. I'm fine." I tried to focus on my friend's voice. I took a breath. "How's Christian?"

"Christian? Hah." Bryan's bark of a laugh made me lift an eyebrow. "That dick is exactly the same as he's always been. A dick."

I took a deep breath, glad to be talking about anything other than how I was feeling or the Rosebriar Room. Even if that meant talking about one of Bryan's numerous exes, male or female. "I mean, ya'll weren't exclusive, right, but last I heard you were all about 'that dick.'"

I looked down at my hands folded in my lap. They were smallish and constantly in motion. I was never good at sitting still, at just *being*. I'd always been fidgety. I twirled the anchor on my bracelet. At my wrists, the cotton bandages chafed a bit. The cuff of my sleeve was tinged slightly pink. I wished I'd changed my shirt before I left the apartment. I was still dressed for work.

"We don't have to talk about Christian."

"I'm curious." I met his eyes. "And I could use the distraction, honestly."

"Well, no. We were definitely not exclusive. Or even really a thing. You know? We started hanging out after Fiona and I broke up."

"That's right. Fiona. I forgot about her." When Bryan and I had first met, he had been dating Fiona. She was a badass. A drummer. She was the epitome of cool. Though it must be said, Bryan was pretty cool himself. An artist, Bryan had met her when he designed the album cover for

Fiona's band, Deathless Eagle. I never listened to the album, *Dowager*, but Bryan had been a fan.

"How could you forget about Fiona? Love that girl." And there it was. A familiar yet sudden, deep stab of envy. Bryan and Fiona had ended things and stayed friends. They stayed a part of each other's lives.

When Kenny and I broke up, so did my whole goddamn world. We decidedly had *not* stayed friends. Did some part of me wish that wasn't the case? I don't know. Maybe then I wouldn't be walking around with the emotional equivalent of a gaping abscess in my gut. Would things be better if Kenny and I still talked? Would things be better if I could say out loud "love that guy" without choking back sobs? After everything that had happened, given who he was with now, I don't know if staying close with my ex would be better for me or not. I *did* know that hearing Bryan talk about how close he and Fiona still were made me want to slam my head against the dashboard. Repeatedly.

"I forgot you guys were still close." I reached and turned the volume up on the radio. After a moment more, Bryan turned it off.

"I feel like we should talk about—"

"I don't want to talk about Kenny."

"I was gonna say about what happened at the Rosebriar," Bryan said carefully. "Maisey didn't give me the details, but she said you were attacked?" I could feel my face turn red, feel the heat in my ears. After a long moment, Bryan asked, "Do you...would you rather talk about Kenny?"

"No! Dude. No. And I sure as hell don't want to talk about the Rosebriar." I tugged down the sleeves of my jacket.

"You keep doing that."

"What?"

"Tugging on your sleeves."

"No, I don't. Shouldn't your eyes be on the road?"

A *ding* from Bryan's phone notified of a potential rider. With a quick jab of his finger, he poked the phone's screen, then swiped away the notification, exiting the app.

"My eyes are on the road." He changed lanes and the car was now driving east toward Lakeshore Drive. "You don't want to talk about Kenny. You don't want to talk about the thing at work. What do you want to talk about? Huh?"

"I dunno."

"No? Well, let me tell you, buddy, you need to start talking about"—without removing his eyes from the road, he gestured toward my wrists—"what happened because, if you'll recall, I was there. Okay? I was there. I was there, and we still haven't fucking talked about *that*!"

As we merged into the swiftly moving traffic of Lakeshore Drive, we started driving faster and faster, heading north. Lake Michigan spread out to the east of us, stretching to the horizon, still except for ripples and the gentle lapping of the lake's waves. It was easier to look out at the water than think too much about the conversation that was happening in the car.

"I said thank-you already!"

"This isn't about 'thank-you!' Okay, this is about—"

"Look, I'm sorry! I'm sorry I put you in that position. That's a shitty thing for a roommate to do, it's just—"

"'A shitty thing for a *roommate* to do'? Are you fucking kidding me? Gabe. Seriously. At this point I would say... I'd like to say that we were friends. Not just *roommates*. And no. It is not just some 'shitty thing.'

Okay? I just want us to be able to talk about it." Swiftly, Bryan pulled off the drive, rapidly taking us down one of the lanes that spiral into the green expanse of Lincoln Park.

"What do you want me to say?"

The car slammed to a stop. Bryan had pulled into a parking spot. We idled there in a lonely stretch of asphalt surrounded by trees. In the distance, joggers ran. They sporadically spotted the transitioning fall greenery of the park with their ugly-ass, expensive, fucking Day-Glo workout wear.

"I'm sorry that I don't have it as easy as you do, Bryan. I'm sorry my dating pool isn't as fucking expansive as, what?—*any* guy or girl in the tri-city area? That—that—that I'm limited to guys. Nope, not just guys but specifically gay guys. And nope, not just gay guys, but only the gay guys who aren't shitty racists. I'm *so* fucking sorry that, when after a goddamn-billion-fucking years, when I finally found the one guy that seemed to deem me worthy of loving, after finding a needle in a fucking haystack, when all of that fucking fell apart on me that—that—that..." I couldn't get the words out. They had all started pouring from my mouth like molten bile I couldn't swallow down anymore, and now there were no more words, just heaving breaths. I could feel the tears running down my face. My shoulders shook as though I had transformed into some inconsolable child. Through the curtain of my tears, I was vaguely aware of Bryan shutting the car off and turning to face me.

I couldn't look at him. I brought my hands to my eyes. It was an impulse, as if I could hold the tears inside my head if I could only close my eyes tight enough. Maybe if I flattened my palms into my eye sockets just right, I could stop this hot, humiliating flood pouring down my stupid face.

Bryan's hand touched gently on my shoulder. "It's okay."

"No. It's not. It wasn't...I didn't..." I wanted to tell him. I wanted to say the words. *It was a mistake. I didn't mean to kill myself. Not really. I was drunk and feeling melodramatic.* But I couldn't. I couldn't say those words. Not out loud. Not yet.

I don't remember him finding me, but that's what happened. After, he hadn't asked any questions and I hadn't provided any answers. He must have been curious as to why I'd been cleared to come home so soon; I hadn't needed to explain to him how I'd convinced the doctors it was all a drunken misunderstanding, and that no, I wouldn't try again.

The weight of Bryan's hand lifted from my shoulder. "I was so scared." It was almost a whisper, he said it so quietly. Almost as if it wasn't something I was meant to hear.

I took a deep breath, then wiped the tears from my face. In the driver's seat, Bryan had turned away. His hands sat limply on the steering wheel. "I'm sorry," I said again.

"I was so scared." He met my gaze. "And I don't want you to say sorry. That's not...you're my friend..."

"Yes."

"You're my friend and...and...you almost died."

"I guess."

"No. It's not a guessing thing. It's a fact. I was there. I saw it all. When the EMTs came and—and—and I rode with you in the ambulance...dude. There was a moment when—" Bryan got really quiet. He lowered his hands from the wheel. Bryan clasped them together in his lap. He cracked his knuckles. It was a nervous habit of his I'd only seen once or twice. The night he broke up with Fiona for one. "There was a moment, Gabe, when I looked at you there on the stretcher and...you were so still. Pale. Your chest wasn't moving and that beepy thing, the—the thing..."

"The EKG monitor?"

"Yeah. That. Gabe, your heart stopped, and they had to use the—"

"The defibrillator?"

"I knew that one," he snapped. "I'm not an idiot."

"Sorry. I didn't mean to—"

"No, I know. It's just...I need you to understand that I get it. I do. I see how much all this shit with Kenny fucked you up. I see it." He didn't look at me. "But it's not worth it." Bryan's eyes were fixed straight ahead, focused on something out beyond the windshield. I looked at his profile. In his eyes, I could see tears starting to glob together like when you fill up a glass of water too much, and the surface tension is the only thing that keeps it from spilling all over the place. He took a deep breath. The car was quiet, and in the silence, I looked at my friend.

"I know it's not. And..." I hadn't even said these words to Maisey. "And I need you to know nothing like that is going to happen again. What I did...it was a mistake." Bryan turned to look at me. His expression was what I could only interpret as some mix of hope and *You've got to be fucking kidding me.* "I was drunk...really, really drunk and in a bad place. A really bad place."

"Really?"

"Yes." But as I sat there, part of me had to wonder. "I mean..."

"Gabe..."

"It *was* a mistake. And...I can't say I'm in that much better of a place now...especially today..." I was rambling. There was something I needed to articulate, but I couldn't find the words. "But that night...it was a sad, dumb, drunk mistake of a thing I did, and really, truly...I don't want to die." I took a deep breath. "But that night...part of me did."

"I—"

"In that moment. Part of me did. And...I don't think I'll ever really be able to thank you enough for being there. Because, even if that part isn't entirely gone, there's more to me than that. Even though everything is awful and hurts and—today especially—my life seems to be shit...I don't want to die, and if it weren't for you...I'd never have gotten the chance to realize that."

Bryan reached across the front seat of the car and pulled me into a hug.

Chapter Fifteen

The rhythm of Bryan's breathing against my shoulder washed over me. It was calming. It was like the subtle in and out of Lake Michigan's waves, slapping against the shore. The weight of his arms clasped around me. The warmth of his body. I sniffed loudly. To add to all the humiliation and tears, my nose was running. There was nothing sexy about the feeling of Bryan's body against mine. But it was nice. More than nice. It reminded me of being small and allowing my dad to wrap me in his arms. I remember being little, lying on my father's chest as he took a nap after work before dinner. I remember hearing his heartbeat. I remember feeling safe. There in Bryan's car, I wiped the tears from my face. A flood of gratitude washed over me.

We sat there in silence for a second before Bryan gave in to his urge to break it. "So...that Tasha girl was a trip, huh?"

I couldn't help but laugh.

"What?" he asked.

"Nothing."

He smiled and turned the key in the ignition with a click. As the car dinged awake, he lowered the window. "I just feel embarrassed I guess." I followed his lead and lowered the window on my side too. The fresh air was chilly on my wet face. "Is it okay if we just stay parked here for a minute?"

"Of course." Bryan turned the car off again. He took a moment before he spoke again. "And you don't need to be embarrassed." Adjusting in his seat, he turned to face me, his legs folded under him in the driver's seat with his back to the window. Casually, he dropped the keys in the cup holder before leaning back.

"Alas, mon frère, being embarrassed is my lot in life." Whatever tears remained on my face were drying rapidly. I laughed at myself. It definitely seemed as though my life was one long train of awkwardness and embarrassments, but that wasn't necessarily a bad thing. The memory of Rod's mouth on mine leapt to the top of my mind. "Shit, I didn't get a chance to tell you…"

"Tell me what?" Bryan looked at me expectantly. He was starting to smile in a curious way that made me feel flushed and stupid. "Dude, are you blushing?"

"Did I ever mention Rod?"

"Rod? The chef-dude from work? Yeah, man."

"He kissed me. Today. At work."

"No fucking way! Was he the one that attacked you?" Instantly aggressive, defensive even, Bryan sat up straight behind the steering wheel. "That's so fucked up!"

"No! No! This was after…all of that." Had it all really been that morning? It hadn't even been a full day yet, but fuck, it seemed like a week had passed. More. In the distance, a guy was running through the park. Despite the chill of the afternoon, he ran shirtless, wearing shorts that revealed his thighs, thick and muscular. He was pale. He was still far away. In the distance, his white skin reflected the daylight diffused by the gray sky above.

"Damn, dude." I could practically hear the gears turning in Bryan's head as he processed the information. A smirk snuck across his face. "How was it?" From over the green lawn of the park, the athletic jogger moved down the running path. He didn't have to be close for me to be able to tell he was fit. A shock of blond hair was blown back by the wind. He looked like a man made of marble.

"It was...pretty hot, if I'm being honest."

"I'll bet. The dude's name is literally a synonym for cock." Laughing, I looked over at my friend.

"Dude! Vulgarity!" Bryan started laughing too. Both of us lost it. I struggled for breath. My body heaved with laughter in a way it hadn't done in ages, and once more, tears squeezed out of my eyes.

"We're just talking about guys! It's okay!"

"Oh, is it?"

"Sure! You're allowed to be vulgar if you're talking about men." Bryan was catching his breath. With a finger he wiped a laugh-tear from the corner of his eye.

"If you say so." Nearer than before, the jogger had stopped.

"That's how karma works! For all the objectifying straight men do of women, it's only fair for us guys to objectify them back a little bit! You know they'd do the same! It's one of the perks of being into guys."

"I'm not so sure..."

"I mean, that's just like the rules of feminism."

"Enough with the *Mean Girls* quotes."

"What? It's been playing on cable all week." I laughed and looked at the expanse of the park. The jogger wasn't close enough for me to make out his face exactly, but I could see his head turn toward the car. It happened subtly. Gradually. His body was still facing the direction he had been running in before, but he'd begun to crane his neck around until I could tell his gaze had locked on us.

"Bryan?" Incrementally, the runner rotated the rest of himself toward the car.

"I mean, like, take for instance that dude over there. Shirtless runner guy? We can talk about how hot he is because he's not a girl. It'd be creepy and gross if we were ogling a female runner, but since it's a guy, it's okay."

"Bryan. Start the car."

"Lighten up. I'm only kidding...kind of." He looked at me with concern. "What's wrong?" In my chest, my heart seemed to beat in slow motion. The jogger had started moving toward us. Bryan followed my gaze. "What's that guy doing?" The jogger broke into a full-on sprint.

"Bryan, start the car!" Next to me, Bryan shoved his hands into the tight space of the cupholder, scrambling for the keys. "Bryan?" The man was approaching rapidly.

As he got closer, I could see his face more clearly. Handsome features had been contorted into a wild grin. The veins in his neck strained, pulsing as his arms and legs pumped. "Bryan, hurry, hurry, hurry—" I couldn't get any other words out of my mouth.

Out of nowhere, the car radio burst to life. The sound of static blared into lyrics though the voice sounded wrong. At first, a familiar voice started to gurgle. The words were distorted, the voice deeper, gravelly. It took me a moment to recognize the voice of Sting, twisted and only barely identifiable. The lyrics of "Every Breath You Take."

"Hurry up!"

"Fuck! I'm trying!"

He managed to get the keys out of the stupid fucking cupholder and jam them into the ignition. The car jumped to life. I shoved my fist against the radio, desperate to silence the awful, hell-dimension Sting blaring from the speakers. In my hand, the dial of the radio spun on its own. It twisted in my hand as if an invisible force were wrenching the dial in the opposite direction. A whir of static and voices rapidly turned to another familiar tune. *Had a sweetheart once I loved, and I was happy as could be; but now he's gone and left me here for someone else, you see. I ain't got nobody, and nobody cares for me. That's why I'm sad and lonely—* It was the same old-timey song from earlier. The one Uber-passenger Tasha had identified as "I Ain't Got Nobody (And Nobody Cares For Me)." Only this time, it wasn't the voice of Ted Lewis singing—it was my own.

But that was impossible. All this was impossible. I battered my hand against the radio console, but the song just played louder and louder. My own voice sounded from the speakers: louder, cheery, twisted, and melodic at first. *Had a sweetheart once I loved... but now he's gone and left me... that's why I'm sad and lonely...* As the song continued to blare, it got louder and louder until I could hear my own voice no longer singing but screaming in fury and pain *That's why I should just fucking die, just fucking kill myself, slit my wrists, just fucking DIE DIE DIEDIEDIE—*

There was a crashing thud as the jogger slammed his fists into the hood. Through our open windows, I could hear his breathing, ragged and heavy. From somewhere deep in his throat, a guttural laugh croaked out. It was an animal sound. With a nightmarish elegance, he began to climb onto the hood of the car. Through the windshield, his eyes never left mine.

Bryan kicked the car into reverse, and we shot back, forcing the jogger to fall off the hood. We accelerated in reverse down the empty lane through the park. Bryan had craned his neck to look behind us as he drove, but I couldn't pry my eyes from the jogger. He had rolled backward, head over heels, and landed on all fours. Now he crouched there, like an animal, eyes on me. We put more and more distance between us. From halfway across the lot, I could see his body coil up as he prepared to launch himself toward the car like a sprinter at the starting blocks. Or a snake readying to strike. Bryan hit the brakes. The car started to spin across the asphalt, and I lost view of the jogger. With a hard yank, Bryan shifted gears and we drove forward, faster and faster. Fixing my eyes on the rearview mirror, I watched as the jogger sprinted after us. As we sped away, he got smaller and smaller. The distorted song blaring from the radio was drowned out by a wave of static. It got more and more quiet until the sound faded to nothing.

"What the fuck?" Bryan cried, eyes frantically alternating between the rearview mirror and the road ahead.

Bryan's hands were wrapped tightly around the steering wheel. His knuckles had grown pale, the tendons pulling tight. His arms were extended to their full length, and his eyes, wide and unblinking, darted between the road and the rearview mirror as he sped out of the park's winding interior lanes.

"Holy shit." The phrase came from my mouth more of a whisper than anything else. I took a deep breath.

"Is he still chasing us?"

"No... I don't think so. No."

Bryan pulled into traffic at a healthy speed, easing his foot off the gas. "Was that the guy that attacked you?"

"No. That guy is in a coma."

"Did you know him? The runner?"

"No. Never seen him before in my life."

"Then why would he just fucking charge the car like that, man?"

"I...I don't know!"

"What aren't you telling me?"

"This morning...and since...shit. Bryan. Things have been weird."

"No shit!" Bryan was scared. Fuck, I was scared.

We kept driving north. Up Clark Street. Whenever I looked over at Bryan, his eyes were either fixed dead ahead on the road or scanning the people on the sidewalks, ready to react at the first sign of danger. "Gabe, what the fuck is going on?"

"I—I, I don't know. And if I did try to explain...you wouldn't believe me if I told you." I had gotten lucky once. Maisey had listened to my story without thinking I'd completely lost it. She hadn't questioned my sanity. I knew I wasn't nuts, and she had accepted that without hesitation. The chances that Bryan would so easily throw out the rules of logic were slim to none.

"How about giving me the fucking benefit of the doubt? We were just attacked by the fucking marathon man back there, and then my car radio went all *Christine* on us..." He immediately met my gaze, earnest and pleading. "You have to give me some fucking context, man."

Where to fucking start? How to fucking start? "I...I..." It was so much easier with Maisey. The story. Everything that had happened. I had needed to tell her so badly that I hadn't thought twice about how to say it all. But now, with the adrenaline still coursing through my veins, I didn't know what to say.

"Start at the beginning." He said it tentatively, gently. "Please?"

"This morning...I went to work." I faltered. It was as though I had something stuck in my throat. It was hard to swallow. "The Sentinel Club is a creepy fucking place."

"Yeah. Nice. But creepy."

"Right. I'd heard stories from people. Thought I'd seen things, heard things, felt things..." Bryan's words rang in my head. *Nice. But creepy.* So many things can be nice and creepy. Pretty and deadly. Alluring and destructive. All at the same time. "I hadn't been back since before..."

"Yeah."

"Well, I dunno. I just went about opening like I normally do..."

"And? Gabe. What happened?"

"We opened for breakfast service, and this guy came in. He...he lost it. Snapped. I don't know. He attacked me. But it wasn't just that. The things he did? It wasn't possible. You know the tables we have in the Rosebriar Room?"

"The big-ass wooden ones?"

"Yeah. He lifted it over his head like it was nothing. He threw it so hard it fucking crashed out the window and landed on Michigan Avenue."

"How?"

"I don't know! But it wasn't just that. It was his voice. The way he moved. The way his body twisted...I can't even describe it."

"I think I get the picture."

"And ever since? Weird shit has been happening. All day. I've gotten strange phone calls...stuff has been moving around on its own...then that guy..." It was all so much. I sunk down into the passenger seat. Breathing became harder. I turned my face toward the open window and inhaled a gust of cold November air.

"This is all so crazy."

"I know. But you have to believe me. I'm not insane. I'm not crazy. I'm not—I'm not making this up."

"I believe you. Fuck!" With one hand he pointed through the windshield at two deep, fist-sized dents in the hood of his car. "How could I *not* believe you?" Bryan continued to drive. I looked over at him, grateful. "But what does it all mean?"

"I don't know." The car moved north through the city. We drove up Clark, passing by the L & L Tavern on the corner of Belmont. It was the same dive bar that both John Wayne Gacy and Jeffrey Dahmer were said to have once frequented. It creeped me out. I'd always refused to go in there, even on the Haunted Ghost Tour of Chicago my sister and I had gone on together a couple of Halloweens ago. I hadn't thought about that tour in years. But as the faded-green bar sign *whooshed* past the car window, something the tour guide had said jumped out from my memory. "I was told this story once..."

"What kind of story?"

"It was on one of those Chicago ghost tours. You know? Where they drive you around on a big black school bus?

"Right, and they're always stopping at different places, yeah?"

"Yeah, at spots all around the city that are supposed to be haunted, telling you stories along the way. There was this one story..."

"What was the story?"

"You know the Hull House, down on Halsted, by UIC?"

"Yeah. I don't know much about it. But I've heard of it before. So?"

"Our tour guide had said one of the people on their tour came back. They took the tour a second time."

"Is that weird?"

"I dunno. I mean, it doesn't sound too strange. But the tour guide said this dude was different the second time around. On edge right from the start. Apparently, the first time they'd gone to the Hull House...something followed him home."

"What the fuck is that supposed to mean? A ghost or something?"

"I don't know. Some kind of entity or something. The tour guide was pretty vague. But she said *it* followed him home after the tour, and the only way for him to get rid of *it* was to go back there again. To leave *it*—or whatever— back where it came from."

I hadn't thought about the story in years. At the time, I couldn't help but wonder what that must be like. To die and become a ghost. To be so lonely floating around in the afterlife you'd be compelled to follow someone home. And after all that, to be returned again. To be left behind again. I remember thinking: *How sad.* But if I knew anything, it was that whatever was following me around didn't *feel* lonely or sad. Every encounter I'd had with whatever it was that seemed to be fixated on me made me believe that this *force* was nothing but hateful. Hateful and destructive. And angry.

"Is that what you think is happening to you? Some entity is following you around?"

How was I supposed to answer that? I knew how it sounded. I looked over at Bryan. I could tell he was freaking out, and I couldn't blame him. Hell, I'd been freaking out all morning. I knew the feeling. I hated it. I felt powerless and scared and confused, and it was time to do something about it.

"Turn around."

"Huh?"

"Turn the car around." I had an idea.

"What are you talking about?"

"Head back down Clark, back the way we came." Bryan did as I asked. "Here. Okay, turn left at the light on Belmont."

We drove past the huge marble expanse of Our Lady of Mount Carmel, the big Catholic church that found itself right at the heart of Boystown. Between Halsted and Broadway on Belmont, the connected complexes of the church and adjoining school spread out with archways, statues, cloisters, and fountains.

"Pull up right here." Bryan pulled the car up just past and across from the church on the south side of the street. "Thanks." I hopped out of the car.

"Gabe. What are you doing?"

"I need more information."

"Are you sure?" I looked across the street at the church, then turned my glance to the low, plain cement building a couple of storefronts down. The Boystown branch of the Chicago Public Library—the Merlo Branch—sat there, waiting.

"Yeah, I'm sure." He looked at me, doubtful. "Well, about as sure as I can hope to be right now." Watching for traffic, I dashed across the street to the library. I turned back to look at Bryan one last time. "Thanks!" I shouted. It was dumb, but it was all I could think to say.

Chapter Sixteen

As soon as I made my way past the first set of thick, heavy glass doors, the temperature warmed. Piles of *The Windy City Times, The Reader, New City*, and other free newspapers sat wilting in a line of stacks, leading from the door of the vestibule to the library itself. Back when I lived off the Red Line, I would come into this branch every so often. Since I'd moved out to Logan Square, I hadn't been back.

The last time I was here had been with Kenny. We had spent hours browsing the books and spinning the towers of borrowable movies, enjoying the nostalgic act of picking out an actual DVD to take home and watch on the couch. I would always want some campy B-movie horror flick from the '80s. He'd always want to watch *Contact.* No matter how many times we'd seen it before. He loved that Jodie Foster movie from the '90s. I could never see the appeal. We usually compromised with old seasons of some TV show or another. Back then, I was still living in my studio apartment, and we'd curl up on my bed across from the television. We hadn't moved in together yet.

In the vestibule the warmth had become stifling. It was easier to breathe inside the library itself. These sorts of buildings never change. The carpeting was the same sort of flat, speckled gray and blue that was in almost every public elementary school in America. Overhead, white fluorescent lights buzzed.

"Hi. How's it going today?" Behind the check-out desk, a guy around my age smiled. His long, straight black hair hung almost to his shoulders.

"That is a loaded question." I could feel the tension in my neck and back. There was a slight tremor in my hands. I shoved them in my pockets.

"Oh? I tried to smile back. His left eyebrow arched inquisitively. Without breaking eye contact, he added a paperback romance novel onto a stack of books. Pictured on the cover, a glistening, well-oiled, well-muscled man with flowing blond hair looked out into the distance as cherry blossoms floated down from the trees around him. My line of vision must have been obvious. "Ah, yeah," he said, picking up the paperback again. "These sorts of books are the kind that gets checked out the most." I rushed to avert my eyes from the bulging pecs on the book cover.

"Yeah?"

"Yeah. I mean, I get it. Who can resist when the cover art is so—" He laughed at himself as he searched for the right word. "—appealing?"

"I guess." My cheeks went hot. I could only imagine how dumb I looked. Blushing at some cute librarian flashing a romance novel in my face. I thought back to the jogger and to the man from the morning. They'd been cute too. The heat in my face evaporated.

"It's crazy. They're all the same. Same hot white dude on the cover. Same descriptions of velvety members and heaving bosoms. Read one and you've read them all." He smiled again. I couldn't help it. I smiled back. He was funny. He was cute. Something about the simplicity of his small talk put me at ease.

"Read a lot of romance novels, do you?"

"From time to time." He looked at the book in his hands. "But only when one catches my eye. I have discerning tastes." I looked at the title: *Love and the Rising Sun*. "I snagged this one from the new release shelf when we first got it. Since then"—he scanned the barcode on the inside cover and dashed his eyes to the computer screen—"it's been checked out over twenty times."

"Any good?"

He laughed and brought his eyes back to mine. They were a rich brown. The color of polished chestnut. "If you like your romance with a splash of not-so-subtle racism."

"I can't say I do."

"Me neither. I picked up *Love and the Rising Sun* more out of a sense of morbid curiosity than anything else."

"And?"

"What do you think?" He said it almost as a challenge. There wasn't anyone else in this part of the library. The guy must have been bored, and I experienced an unexpected surge of gratitude for boredom. He smiled at me expectantly. I looked at the cover.

"Um, shirtless blond guy shows up on some sort of...expedition...?"

"He's the captain of a trade ship," he confirmed.

"And after landing in...Japan?"

"Yeah."

"He falls in love with a sexy and mysterious Geisha..." I continued.

"Bingo!"

"Who, um...manages to quell his wanderlust."

He smiled again. "You're good at this."

"Read one and you've read them all." I was embarrassed to admit it, but I had read my share of awful romance novels. Though, it would probably be more appropriate to say I'd skimmed them, as opposed to actually having read many such novels start to finish. The truth is, I'd usually flip through most of the pages, scanning the prose for any hint of an oncoming sex scene. Then, having done so, I would promptly return the book to whatever display I'd grabbed it from.

When I was young, on the verge of puberty, those trashy paperbacks were my first real encounters with sex. On family trips to the grocery store, I'd wander off to the book and magazine aisle of the Jewel and have at it. Magazines were too risky. The images too obvious. There was a level of deniability to the black-and-white text-covered pages of a novel. Reading the description of a man's body, as opposed to openly admiring an image of one, seemed safer. It was like hiding in plain sight. It was a simpler time. Back then, before I was brazen enough to dig up actual porn on the family computer, I was at least able to flip to the very kind of word-porn descriptions of "velvety members and heaving bosoms" this librarian was poking fun at.

"Ah, so you're one of my tribe then, huh?" He tilted his head slightly as though trying to place me from somewhere.

"Tribe?"

"A hopeless romantic. At least that's what my boyfriend calls me. He's a bit of a skeptic, but they say opposites attract, so..." I forced myself to break eye contact. I hadn't even realized it, but our short exchange had started something within me. Our simple back and forth, the small kindness of human connection with this guy, had started to inflate a tiny balloon of...what? Hope? A sense of potential for...something. And with a single word—*boyfriend*—the balloon popped. I tried to laugh, hoping it wouldn't sound as pathetic as I now felt.

"Yeah, I guess I'm pretty hopeless." A moment of silence dragged on for what seemed like forever.

"I get it." I looked up. "Well, I'm Stephen," he said, pointing to his nametag. "Let me know if I can help you find anything."

"Thanks." I took a deep breath. I turned, about to head into the depths of the library when I was struck with a sobering realization: I had no clue where to start. I was at a total loss for how to begin the search I'd come here to do. All of a sudden, the quiet became suffocating. The number of books, the amount of information, the magnitude of it all overwhelmed me.

"Actually, there is something you could help me with."

"Yeah?" What could I say that wouldn't sound completely unhinged? Boyfriend or not, the idea of coming across like a crazy person to this cute librarian made me want to swim out into the middle of Lake Michigan with a cinder block tied to my ankles. No. I couldn't mention any of the crazy shit that had happened. "Uhh...what might that be?" I was taking too long to think of something to say.

"History." The word leapt out of my mouth.

"History."

"Yeah. Um...local history. Like of Chicago." My mind kicked into gear again. "Specifically of downtown."

"Yeah, we can definitely help you out with that. Was there something specific like a time period or something we could narrow it down to?" I racked my brain for the trivia our managers had forced all the hosts to learn about the hotel. The information had never been too in depth; just a list of factoids deemed compelling enough to satiate your average guest with an interest in architecture.

"Maybe something around the time of the World's Fair? And the um, the old private clubs."

"Like the Cliffdwellers, University Club, the Chicago Athletic Association?" I nodded as he rattled off the names. "The Sentinel Club." My breath caught on my lips. I froze. The nodding stopped. It was an instinctual reaction. "You okay?"

"Yeah. Yes. I'm fine." The concern in his kind eyes made something in my chest relax just the slightest bit. I forced myself to breathe. *Just act fucking normal!* "Thanks. That's the exact sort of information I'm looking for."

"Sure thing." Stephen turned again to the computer. He typed something, then clicked around with the PC's mouse. A small receipt printer next to the monitor buzzed to life, and a long strip of thin paper spooled into Stephen's hand. "If you go up the stairs and head towards the North East corner of the library, you'll find our section on local history." He ripped the receipt from the printer and handed it to me. "Here's a list of books you might find helpful." He smiled again. "Some sort of research project?"

"Something like that." I skimmed my eyes over the reading list. Hopefully, one of these books would give me some sort of information, which would shed some light on what was happening. I looked at Stephen. He was so friendly. So willing to help. Part of me wanted to ask him to print another list; one with books about hauntings or demons, spirits, the supernatural. Anything that might apply to the fucked-up things I'd been experiencing. But I couldn't do that. I'd seem like a freak.

"Anything else I can help you with?"

"Uh...actually..." This was my chance. Bryan and Maisey had both believed me. A desperate part of me hoped maybe Stephen would too. Maybe he'd help me overcome whatever fucking nightmare entity had been making my life a scene from *Poltergeist* and then leave his boyfriend, marry me, and we'd go on to grow old together after raising our adopted children and assortment of dogs in a nice townhouse in Andersonville. None of those things would happen if he thought I was a psychopath. Not to say any of those things would happen anyway. No. I couldn't tell him. There was no way to ask for the sort of help I really needed.

"Yeah?"

"Yeah." I needed to say something. Anything. "I guess I was just wondering...what was it that made you so morbidly curious about *Love and the Rising Sun?*"

"Well, my dad's Japanese and my mom is Korean, so...I guess, I was just in the mood to be angry." He laughed, then shook his head as if to dismiss the thought.

"I get that."

"Really?" I reached over to the stack of paperbacks sitting on the counter. Careful to not knock the whole stack over, I pulled a novel I'd noticed from the middle of the pile and handed it to Stephen. "*Passion Amongst Pistoleros?*" On the cover, a blonde woman with enormous breasts clung to the muscular brown chest of a mustachioed sombrero-wearing bandito. This was one of those sorts of novels I'd actually read the entirety of.

"The cover caught my eye when I was browsing down at the Harold Washington Branch. Started flipping through, and before I knew it, I'd read the whole damn thing."

"Morbid curiosity?"

"Morbid curiosity," I agreed. "And the same sort of urge to feel angry, I guess."

I remembered reading it among the shelves of the library downtown. The stereotypes and clichéd portrayal of Mexicans in the book pissed me off. The objectification of the characters. Awful caricatures of these lawless brutes fueled solely by passion. It made me have flashbacks to all the guys I would hook up with or try to date before Kenny. White dudes who'd call me "guapo" or "papi." Guys who'd try and start flirty conversations with me by saying how much they "like Latin guys" or how much they don't, but how there was something about me that made them want to make an exception.

It made me angry at myself, too, for the times I'd go along with it. The times I got a sick sort of pleasure out of being objectified. The times I craved any attention I could get even if it was the kind that positioned me as some exotic sexual novelty as opposed to a goddamn human being. Reading *Passion Amongst Pistoleros*, consuming the words by and for these straight white ladies as they described some Mexican man's dick: being outraged by it, turned on by it, and feeling guilty for it. I remember trying to talk about it with Kenny. He thought I was being ridiculous. Oversensitive.

"Yeah."

"Well, thanks again." I skimmed my eyes down the reading list. Turning away from the desk, I made my way for the stairs.

"Hey, uh...sorry, I didn't catch your name. Wait a second..." My heart fluttered briefly. I hadn't made it very far from the desk and already he was calling me back.

"Gabe," I said, turning to face him again. "My name's Gabe."

"Gabe. Keep an eye out for Kyle. He's upstairs shelving right now."

"Kyle?"

"Kyle Shafer. He's one of the other librarians here, and he's also a bit of a local historian. One of his books is actually on the list, uh..." Stephen stepped out from around the counter and came near, taking my hand in his. He pulled the list and my hand closer so he could get a better view and skimmed the titles, looking for something. His hand on mine was soft, yet firm. Warm. "*Boystown and Beyond: Unearthing Chicago's Hidden Queer History.*" He released my hand and moved back toward his post behind the counter. I took my time exhaling and refocused.

"Upstairs?"

"Yeah. He's the older African American guy. Really knows his stuff." He smiled again. I had no clue who the fuck Stephen's boyfriend was, but I envied him. And hated him.

"Thanks. I...I really appreciate it." I started to walk up the stairs.

"No problem!" With a friendly wave, Stephen went back to whatever it was he had been doing when I first walked in the library. I returned the wave, but by then he wasn't looking.

Chapter Seventeen

I don't know what it is I love about public libraries. It's definitely not the weird old guys watching porn at the public-use computers. It's not the smelly bathrooms. Not napping homeless people. Maybe it's nostalgia. The butterflies in my stomach hadn't changed from the ones I used to get as a kid walking past the rows and rows of books.

There are so many stories, and I could pick up any one of them. I could grab one, read it, and be transported into someone else's adventure. Someone else's head. Someone else's skin. But those adventures weren't real. They were stories. They were safe. Real life is its own adventure in which the dangers aren't fiction. The hard truth is, adventures are a lot less fun when the dangers aren't pretend. It's an entirely different thing to have to walk through the world where people seem to hate you, want to hurt you...and why? For being who you are.

It helped me to breathe easier just being in the library, surrounded by books in the kind of familiar place some part of me registered as safe. Warily, I looked at the porn dude. He seemed focused on what he was doing. I couldn't help but notice the video featured two Asian women going down on each other. I should have guessed. Of course, the kind of pervy middle-aged man who'd watch porn in the public library would have such specific tastes. I guess even a safe place isn't untouchable.

I looked down at the long strip of receipt paper in my hand. Each book Stephen had put on the list was right on the shelf exactly where it should be. Dragging my finger along the spines of the books, I matched the call number on the paper in my hand to a thick volume. "*Mysterious Chicago: History at Its Coolest* by...Adam Selzer. Check." I piled it on top of the stack of books I'd started to compile in my hands. It was getting heavy, and I had only gathered half of Stephen's suggestions. I made my way over to an empty worktable.

All the books spilled across the table with a crash. The sound echoed loudly, shattering the quiet of the library. In the far computer nook, the older man continued watching his porn, unfazed. Three worktables across from me, a sleeping heap of person continued to doze.

A couple of aisles away, a different librarian looked up from his shelving. Mildly dismayed at the noise, he raised an eyebrow and gave a slight shake of his head, and then he went back to his shelving. He looked to be in his midsixties. At first glance, given his style and his body language, one could easily assume he was gay. He was smartly dressed with thick, yellow plastic-framed glasses, and whether or not such assumptions were appropriate, the librarian's aesthetic was just ostentatious enough to draw attention. Just colorful enough to stand out in a crowd.

The Merlo Branch of the Chicago Public Library was right on the southern edge of Boystown. It was comforting to walk around this part of town and see the rainbow banners hanging from the lampposts and the little flag stickers in the storefronts. It was a part of the city where queerness, however overt or subtle, didn't particularly stand out. It was the norm. Even the shelf the older librarian was reshelving had a large strip of rainbow-patterned poster paper stretched above it, emblazoned with the words LGBTQ+ HISTORY.

What did Stephen say this librarian's name was? Kevin something? Stephen had been really helpful. And frustratingly cute. And he had a boyfriend, so none of those things really mattered. Why should his being in a relationship make me sad and frustrated? I literally had much more important things to worry about. Like the very reason I came to this fucking library in the first place, for instance. I needed to focus. I looked down at the books sprawled in front of me.

I picked up *Mysterious Chicago* and flipped it open randomly. The words filled the page like dead ants lined in a row. With a deep breath, I tried to focus on reading. Under the table my leg started to shake up and down. A nervous habit that emerged when I was impatient or agitated. Coming here had seemed like a good idea. It seemed proactive. But now, even with Stephen's help and all these books in front of me, I was drowning in information. I couldn't breathe. I had no clue where to start.

Impatiently, I flipped to the index at the back of the book. Scanning the rows of listings, I looked for the Sentinel Club. Nothing. "Shit." I grabbed another book and flipped to the index. There, under S was the club. I flipped to the pages listed. Architectural information. Notable members. In the index of the next book, the Sentinel Club came up again. I flipped to the pages, and there was an entry regarding the construction of the club in 1893, which I already knew was right around the time of the construction for the World's Fair. All this stuff was old information I had already been force-fed during host training at the Rosebriar.

Curious tourists and guests of the hotel would always come up to us at the host stand. They'd always ask the same questions. Where's the bathroom? What's the history of this place? Where's the bathroom? So, this used to be a private club, huh? Bathroom? When was this place built? Do you know where the bathroom is? Ad nauseum. When I first started, they gave us a thick packet full of trivia on the hotel/former private men's club. They quizzed us and prepped us on all the information sprinkled throughout the books in front of me. It was a dead end. I was back at square one.

"Goddammit."

Out of the corner of my eye, I thought I caught a glimpse of movement. Over by the computers. Had porn guy turned his attention my way? I glanced over. His eyes were still focused on the screen. Had I imagined it? Was the momentary feeling of being watched all in my head?

Reaching into my pocket, I grabbed my phone. I typed "the Sentinel Club" into the Google search. I scrolled through the Yelp reviews, the hotel's website, menus, and another list of notable members from when the SCC was still a private club: page after page of useless information. Then, finally, after dredging down through countless irrelevant search results, one link in particular stopped me cold. "Death on the Thirteenth Floor."

I clicked the link. It was an article from the '70s about a man, unnamed in the article, who jumped to his death from the thirteenth-floor private dining room of the Sentinel Club. When the club was reopened as the hotel, the dining room had been converted into the Rosebriar Room. The article didn't provide any more information. Apparently, the dead man was an employee of the club. It was ruled a suicide. That was it.

I went back to Google and typed in another search query: death, Sentinel Club, and Chicago. A list of articles popped up. Mostly in digitized archives from *The Tribune* and *The Sun Times*, all going back decades. They featured short vague reports of people dying in the building. Suicides. Accidents. Never names. Almost always service staff at the club. The deaths were sporadic and spread across the years. Given the high profile of the Sentinel Club's members, it made perfect sense why these stories wouldn't have gotten more coverage. The members at the SCC were uniformly rich and connected, and some were the founding members of the same Chicago newspapers I was browsing the archives of right now. Controlling the coverage of these stories would have been nothing.

"Holy shit."

"You all right?" The question startled me out of my chair.

"Fucking hell!" I whirled to face the speaker.

"Sorry, didn't mean to scare you." The other librarian looked at me, concerned. "You done with these books? I can reshelve them for you now, if you are."

"Uh, thanks. Yeah. I am." He pushed the frames of his yellow glasses up the bridge of his nose. "You're Mr....Mr. Shafer, right?"

"I am." I looked at the mess of books I had assembled and reached out to grab *Boystown and Beyond* before he could collect it.

"So, you wrote this?" I realized as I looked down at the cover of the books I'd gone through so far, I had completely ignored this one. Not on purpose really. I hadn't even thought about it. I guess it hadn't really seemed relevant. What did queer history have to do with the Sentinel Club or any of the shit I'd been dealing with?

"I did." He spoke carefully. Suspiciously. He squinted his eyes at me slightly. "Let me guess. Stephen suggested you pick it up," Shafer said, with a tired smile.

I nodded.

He sighed and shook his head. "Nice boy that one. But doesn't know when to quit."

"I don't understand."

With a small chuckle, Shafer sat down across from me. "Stephen seems to think I'm lacking for attention. He's taken to the notion people asking me about my book might...I don't know, liven things up for me a little." He looked at me over the top of his glasses, flirty-like.

I blushed, surprised by a flash of shyness. I looked down at the book in my hands.

Shafer tapped his fingertips against the tabletop. "Don't get old." Delicately, he raised his elbows onto the table. He folded his hands and rested his chin atop them coyly. He smiled, a touch sad. I noticed he wasn't wearing a wedding ring.

"Don't know if I have much say in the matter." I tried to laugh. It came out sounding hollow.

"Well, enjoy your youth while you have it." He looked at me closely. We sat there together for a moment. The silence wasn't uncomfortable, but it was loaded. With a slight squint of his eyes, he asked, "Are you seeing anyone?" His tone seemed honestly curious. I couldn't tell if he was still flirting or not, but the question seemed innocent enough.

"Um, no...I'm not actually. I just got out of a relationship." I lowered my hands beneath the table. These stupid fucking bandages on my wrists. The whole epic fucking embarrassment of what I'd done was like a badge everyone could see. A fucking forehead tattoo reading "Pathetic" would be more subtle. It'd be different if it hadn't all been...what? Such a cliché? If my impulse for self-destruction wasn't so stereotypically linked to a guy, to a broken heart? Perhaps if my pain had some other source, if my issues stemmed from some internal struggle or official diagnosis, I'd feel as though I'd come by my still-healing wrists more honestly. Is "honest" even the right word? "Valid" maybe? Maybe I'd feel less shame about the scars I'd bear for the rest of my life if I hadn't gotten them in a drunken tailspin, brought on by a broken heart. Regardless, I was a fraud. A joke.

"Was he a white boy?" The question took me off guard.

"I'm sorry?"

"Your ex. Didn't end well, I take it. He a white boy?"

"Um, yeah. He was." There was a relief in Shafer's use of the word "he." It meant I didn't have to go through the same tired micro-coming-out I so often had to initiate. It's inevitable when talking with new people. Every so often significant others or exes come up in conversation. So much can be revealed with the use of a single pronoun. Having to decide whether I want to be revealed in such a way is a uniquely exhausting privilege. One I doubt Shafer has dealt with much. Only the most clueless of observers would ever assume he was a straight man. Yet, the privilege of assumed straightness, of "passing," only had value because we've been taught that being straight is somehow better. More and more this idea filled me with a pain and sorrow I struggled to put into words. And I was starting to realize it wasn't the only such idea.

"Dating is harder for us. For you, me, and Stephen even. Not to say there's anything wrong with dating white boys, but...it's hard." It was true. I'd thought as much before. But I don't know if anyone had ever articulated that thought out loud to me until now.

"It is." I wondered if Mr. Shafer had ever voiced these thoughts out loud before either.

"We're either invisible to them, or we're some sort of exotic treat. Meanwhile, everything we see and hear and are told to want places them smack-dab in the middle of the goddamn universe of desirability." I couldn't help but laugh. The sleeper a couple of tables down grumbled slightly in response. "And if you're swishy, or anywhere near as fabulous as I happen to be, forget about it." Shafer pushed his glasses up the bridge of his nose again. He got quiet. Reflective. Maybe even sad. "And when you get old...you might as well be dead." Taking his time, he started to get up. One by one, he collected the books from the table for reshelving.

"That's not why Stephen told me about your book." He looked at me, surprised. "He said you might be able to help me." Shafer smiled. Librarians, or at least good ones, always came to life the most when they could help. Their eyes glow. Shafer was a good librarian.

"How can I help?"

"Well, Mr. Shafer, I—"

"Kyle. Please."

"Kyle. I'm, uh...working on a, um, research project...of sorts."

"I see."

"Do you know anything about the Sentinel Club Chicago?"

Shafer got extremely still. I could see his eyes dart around my face, searching for something. His breathing became ragged. He froze for a second, deliberating. Finally, he sat back down across from me. He scanned the other two bodies on this floor of the library. His eyes lingered on the white man at the computer.

"Why do you want to know about that place?" The tone of his voice sent electricity up my spine. He knew something.

"Research."

"Why?" This time, his voice was forceful. His eyes hardened. I didn't know what to say. I took a deep breath.

"I work there. It's a hotel now."

"I know that." The sweetness in his voice was gone. He didn't sound mean exactly but sharp.

"There's a restaurant. On the thirteenth floor."

"The Rosebriar Room."

"Yes." His eyes never left mine. "I'm a host there."

"And you were there? This morning?"

I didn't answer. I could tell, by the way he looked at me, he knew I had been. He didn't need to say anything else. Neither did I. We sat there in silence. The moment seemed to stretch on for ages.

"Please. I...I need to understand," I said.

He looked at me, then around us again. I hadn't noticed, but the porn watcher had disappeared from the computer area. The sleeper snored a few tables beyond us, obscured beneath layers of soiled clothing. Otherwise, we were alone.

He picked up his book and flipped to the index as I had done with all the other books on Stephen's list, and then he placed the open book in my hands. I scrolled my eyes down the columns of words and page numbers until they landed on what I was looking for. The Sentinel Club Chicago. The trail of numbers next to the SCC's entry was longer than it had been in any other book. I looked up to Shafer who gave me a nod. Flipping through the book, I went to the first page number listed.

An entry on the Legacy Walk in Boystown. I scanned the page. Nothing about the Sentinel Club. Every time I went back to the index and then to the next page number listed, there were pages upon pages on queer artists, activists, and the AIDS crisis but never anything on the Sentinel Club.

"What does this mean?"

Shafer took his glasses off. He set them gingerly on the table and squeezed the bridge of his nose. With a deep breath, he rubbed his eyes and proceeded to return the yellow frames to his face. "This book was a labor of love. I spent years doing research. The good, the bad, and the ugly. I found it all and I put it all in this book." His voice was constrained, and his eyes never left the tome in front of me. "When I got back the manuscript from my editor, I was told all references to the SCC had to be removed."

"What sort of references? I don't understand how a place like the Sentinel Club Chicago connects to"—I flipped to the cover of the book in front of me—"*Chicago's Hidden Queer History.*"

"Exactly." He looked excited and exasperated all at once as he met my gaze. "What do you know about the SCC?"

"Uh, the basics, I suppose? The sort of trivia out-of-towners and the folks on architectural history tours tend to like."

"Mmhmm." He urged me to continue.

"It was built in 1893. It used to be a private men's club. The members were all straight rich white men. You know, the sort of guys who were running the show back then." I looked at my phone sitting on the table next to the books. "And...it's starting to look like a lot of people have died there over the years..."

"Not 'starting to.' It's been looking that way since the beginning." Shafer leaned in. He lowered his voice as if there was someone hidden nearby who might be listening. "People've been dying in that place since it was first built. The thing you need to understand about a place like that is, it's the meeting place of all the worst things in the world."

"Worst things?"

"Power, money, and privilege." A sort of frantic energy began to build in his voice. "They might seem interchangeable, but each one comes with their own nuances. And you better believe straightness and whiteness are often couched in all three." It was as though I'd thrown a log on a flame which had been kindling unattended to for a long time. Here was a subject this man knew a lot about, and he had been dying to share his knowledge. "Now, when the club was first built, the folks who worked there, the staff, tended to be extremely poor. As you might expect. They were mostly Irish, German, and Polish immigrants. Then, starting in 1910, there was a large influx of Mexican folk followed by the large Black populations of the Great Migration around 1916."

"What does this have to do with anything?"

"Everything, child! All those deaths you had popping up when you did your, what, your googling or whatever? Did you think it was the rich-ass white folks dying there in their fancy lounges and private suites? No. It was folks like us. The folks who worked in that building."

"That still do..."

"That still do."

"Are you saying those people were murdered?"

"Some were, some weren't, I reckon. Read a lot about suicides there, didn't you? Well, if you find yourself driven to do something like that as a result of the abuses of your employer and the abuses of power, all at the hands of men who feel like they can treat you however they want, do to you whatever they want…if all that were to drive you—to drive *a person* to end it all—the line between murder and suicide starts to get blurry, don't you think? In my opinion it sure as hell does."

"Abuses?"

"The Sentinel Club wasn't the only private men's club in Chicago at the time."

"Right."

"And all of these men's club allowed for the same sorts of thing. Hell, back then, every other damn storefront on Wabash was either a saloon or a bordello. But for men of power and influence, they didn't have to skulk so low. For them, there were the private clubs. Places for them to socialize exclusively. To wine and dine and indulge. Now sure, those indulgences ran the usual gamut. Booze, drugs, women, gambling. The legality of it never really coming into play because of…"

"The privacy."

"Exactly. The privilege. The money. These men were untouchable. Stories of having secret entrances and stairwells to bring women into all men's clubs were practically public knowledge. But when it came to other men…" Everything he was saying made perfect sense. It all seemed to click with something I'd always suspected.

"So, the Sentinel Club—"

"Functioned as a brothel for rich and powerful men, specifically those interested in other men."

"A private men's club."

"Mmhmm."

"A gay brothel."

"Now, now, I didn't say gay. Just like they wouldn't have said so either. No sir. Those men were as closeted as they were rich, and none of them would have been as self-respecting or self-aware to identify as anything that would threaten their station. Uh-uh. They were men with certain...tastes. Certain proclivities. But what it boils down to is nothing but internalized homophobia, in my humble opinion. You see it all the time, even today. Imagine what it was like back then."

"Holy shit."

"Now you understand why they wouldn't have wanted my research popping up here in my little book. The people that are still big wigs today, the ones still affiliated with the SCC, wouldn't want the legacy of their club tainted by my findings, now would they? So, they made it disappear. I managed to keep the index as it was in the earlier editions. Had a friend at the publisher's, if you know what I mean." He gave me a sly wink, and I couldn't help but smile. "But they caught it in the later editions. Few that there were." If I had stumbled across this book anywhere else, in some bookstore or another branch of the library, even the indexes would have been scrubbed of any reference to the SCC.

"This has to relate to all the deaths in that place. Doesn't it?"

"Well, it was a perfect storm for all sorts of fucked-up shit. As time went on, the place got a reputation. If, as a private club, all that...what's the popular term for it nowadays, not machismo but—"

"Toxic—?"

"Yessir, all the *toxic masculinity,* the self-hate in that place; of course, it would manifest itself in all sorts of evil ways. Some dark shit goes down in places that are private.

I think about all the fucked-up abuses of power that must have gone unchecked for decades, and it makes me sick."

"How do you know all this?"

"Honey, I know all sorts of things. Back in the days when I still fancied myself a writer—I wanted to be an investigative journalist for a time—I made it a point of knowing things. Of collecting stories and information. Often from the sorts of people that go unseen. The sorts of stories that go untold."

"You mean—"

"After I picked up on the lead, I conducted a series of interviews with former staff members from the SCC. The current staff members wouldn't say much. Too close to it. Too shook. But the older folks. They'd seen some shit, and you better believe that, after years of holding on to those secrets, they were ready to talk. They just needed someone to listen."

"What kind of shit?"

"You don't want to know." I thought about what I'd seen so far today. I struggled to breathe for a second, but when I looked at Shafer, I found myself able to inhale again.

"You're probably right. I *don't* want to know. Not really, but..."

"But?" He looked at me with a sense of concern. He seemed to consider something for a moment, then continued. "Let's just say, a fair bit of the *activity* there, if you know what I mean, was decidedly not consensual."

At the other table, the sleeping homeless person gave a grunt. I froze for a second. With a rustle, the person adjusted, pulling back their hood and letting a cascade of beaded braids click against the table. A moment later, a subtle snoring began again.

Shafer dropped his voice to a dire whisper. "I've heard horror stories. Employees and staff members, especially the young, fit black and brown boys working there, were the most vulnerable. If a member took a liking to you, you might as well be theirs. Rape. Assault. Orgies and violence and all sorts of dark business. In the darkness and privacy of those halls, there were no rules. No laws. You weren't a person to them. You were meat. And they treated you as such."

"Fuck." The word slipped from my mouth quietly. A whisper. *You were meat. Meat. You weren't a person. And they treated you as such.* Shafer's words echoed in my head. I knew what that was like.

"You okay, baby?" I could feel the concern in his gaze.

With a quick swipe of my hand, I wiped away an errant tear from my cheek. "Mmhmm."

Gently, Shafer took my hand in his. "Remember, we're talking about the sort of people who didn't have a lot of options." I nodded as he went on. "As I continued my interviews, multiple unverified reports and allegations would arise of human trafficking even. But by the time I was collecting the information, the statutes of limitation had been exceeded in most of the cases, and for the rest, all I had was hearsay."

"I can only imagine all of this went unreported at the time."

"Don't be naive. Just because you're pretty, you got no excuse to play dumb. Of course it went unreported." He smiled wryly and gave me a wink. An attempt to lighten the mood I appreciated greatly.

"Well, what happened with all of this?"

"When I got the notes from my editor, from the publisher, I tried to resist the censorship, but...then all of the freelance opportunities I had as a journalist started drying up. I was by no means in the closet even then, but...times were different. My personal life was personal. So, when I received a letter containing compromising photos of myself and a paramour...I took the hint. I made the edits and redactions. Kept the index as it was as my own little pièce de résistance for as long as it was able to fly under the radar, and that was that. A few years after, I retired from the writing game. And here we are."

"And what about the Sentinel Club? Do you think all this shit is going on still?"

"Oh baby. I don't know. I doubt it. With the change in culture, a lot of other things changed too. I know in the '90s and early 2000s the club was struggling to even attract members. The less exclusive, the less private, the less wiggle room they would have had. At least that's the impression I got. Then when the club ceased operations only to reopen as a hotel...? I don't see how things could still go on the way they used to. But..."

"But what?"

"But things like that leave a mark on a place. All that evil and toxicity; I think—I *believe*—things like that have a certain kind of energy. The kind of energy that stays on like a stain."

I thought back to this morning. Before the events in the Rosebriar Room. I thought about the conversation I had with Ernesto and Sofia. I thought about the vibes I'd gotten in that place. Before all the rest of the fucked-up shit of this morning and since, so much of what Shafer was saying made sense.

"Do you..." The question started to come out of my mouth before I could stop it. "Never mind."

"No. What?"

"I was gonna ask if you believed in—" I took a deep breath. "—the supernatural? Like ghosts and hauntings."

"I don't."

"Right."

"But I do believe in evil." He looked me dead in the eye. "And evil, like the sort of evil that has existed in that place, doesn't just go away. It has implications that reverberate through time. Not in some wishy-washy, boo-says-the-ghost sort of way, no. Nah-uh. But in the sort of ways that can ruin lives and can kill even years after the original sin has been committed. Slavery may be over in this country. But that don't mean Black people aren't still getting killed and incarcerated by the systems slavery built." He took a deep breath and stood. With a pat on my shoulder, he gathered the books he meant to reshelve, then set to work.

Chapter Eighteen

I made my way west down Belmont. Everything Shafer had said made sense. It explained so much about what I'd experienced at the Sentinel Club in The Rosebriar Room. But what about what had been going on since the morning? Shafer didn't believe in ghosts or the supernatural. But there was no natural explanation for the things I'd seen.

Ultimately, I had only checked out one book. The weight of it under my arm was comforting. A heavy, thick hardcover book, *The Encyclopedia of the Paranormal* had to be almost five pounds. Edited by Gordon Stein, PhD, it was the size of a physics textbook. Its heft at least seemed promising. If Shafer was right about the SCC and all the evil shit that had gone down there, he was also right when he said evil leaves a "stain" on the people and places it touches. A stain had been left on the place. I knew that to be true. But what I was still struggling to understand was what exactly all of this had to do with me. Shifting the weight of the book from one arm to the other, I kept walking. The 'L' was only a few more blocks.

The idea of going back to my apartment gave me pause. Walking into those rooms, filled with the reek of rotting plants and the twisted geometrical stacks of furniture, was maybe the last thing I wanted to do. But I could kill some time by riding the Brown Line down through the Loop before taking the Blue Line back toward

Logan Square. By the time I'd get there, Bryan would probably be done driving.

Returning to that empty apartment was more than I could handle on my own. With Bryan there, it would be different, better. Besides, the long train ride would give me time to skim through the tome tucked under my arm. If the massive encyclopedia had any answers or useful tips for ghost proofing my apartment, at the very least I'd be able to take some kind of action once I got there. I needed to do something. Anything. I needed to be proactive. I'd been feeling helpless—hopeless—for so long, it was time to at least try.

I waited at the corner for the walk signal. Across the street was a fancy new ramen restaurant that used to be a bar and previously had been another bar which had been another, different bar before that. There's something about the life of a city. The way a single space, one building, can have so many lives. How is it the past can live on in the walls of a place, remembered by some but completely forgotten by others? How is it something can change, yet stay the same?

I'd been at this corner so many times. I remember when the same space now occupied by this fancy, overpriced noodle spot was a bar called SPIN. They had some of the cheapest drinks you could find, go-go dancers in skimpy underwear, and weekly "shower contests" where bar patrons could win money or drinks by participating in what was basically a wet tighty-whities contest. I remember how the giant posters of guys in jockstraps loudly told passersby just what type of bar it was. Just what sort of neighborhood you were walking into if you chose to continue heading north up Halsted. I remembered strolling by that bar with Kenny when we first started dating. He wouldn't be caught dead inside. He hated coming to Boystown. He hated such blatant expressions of homosexuality. He considered them ostentatious.

At the time, I thought it had to do with the fact that he came from a small town. We'd met the week he moved to Chicago, and I had shown him all my favorite places. We would walk around the city for hours. We'd stroll through parks and stop at cafes and bookstores. I shared the city I loved with him. Now, there wasn't a single place I could go that wasn't stained by him; by my memories with him.

Now, everywhere I went, I expected him to pop up. I could feel myself waiting to run into him. My eyes were constantly scanning crowds for his face. My body was constantly tensing up as though preparing for a blow, expecting to get hit. I'd be constantly tearing myself in two with the desperate desire to see him, and the equally dire need to never set eyes on him again. My instinct for self-preservation was continually warring with some deep, masochistic urge to feel the pain that seeing him would inflict. That's love, I guess.

The light turned green, and I crossed the street. Overhead, the sun was moving steadily westward. The shadows were stretching as the afternoon crawled along. This had to be the longest fucking day of my life. I could feel the exhaustion in my body as I crawled up the stairs to the train platform. I pulled out my phone and checked the time. A quarter to five. Rush hour. Perfect.

The platform was packed. People were just getting off work, heading home. Wearing business suits or khakis. A distracted thirtysomething in a Brooks Brothers jacket looked down at his phone. His blond hair reflected the afternoon sun. It reminded me of the jogger. I averted my eyes just as he looked up from his phone.

The CTA was crowded, and I became instantly aware of how vulnerable I was. Out of the corner of my eye, I kept watch for any sudden movements. I stretched my peripheral vision, seeking out any sign of unwarranted attention. A glance in my direction. A smile. A laugh. Every twitch, every gesture was sending warning signals firing through my nervous system. I was like a rabbit that had stumbled into a fox's den.

The overhead screen reported the next Brown Line headed to the Loop was two minutes away. I focused on breathing. In and out. I tried to remain calm, but the train platform was so crowded with commuters I could barely move. I was adrift in a sea of people, and I was drowning. I was a dog paddling on the surface of rough waters, trying desperately to stay afloat while just below the surface a shark was circling. A mouth full of razor-sharp teeth I couldn't see but somehow knew was there, lurking.

With a rush of sound and wind, the train pulled in. I hadn't realized how close I had gotten to the edge. The force of the rushing train blew my hair back out of my face. I edged backward. The tips of my shoes were just inches from the blue rubberized edge of the train platform. Just inches from the rushing wall of metal. Behind me, I could feel bodies, pressed up against my back, unmoving. Twisting my head around, all I could see were the faces of men. A mass of sandy-blond hair. Blue and green eyes. Reddish stubble. Was that a smile or a widening grin? Was that a causal laugh between fellow commuters or the croaking chuckle that had followed me throughout the day? The train groaned to a quick stop and the doors slid open with a digital ringing sound.

I rushed to enter the southbound Brown Line train. The crowd behind me piled on as well. I looked around, increasingly aware of the fact that I was the only person of color on the train. No one looked my way. I took a deep breath. In the far corner of the car, I noticed a solitary seat empty. The momentum of the train rocked beneath my feet. I made my way over and sat, still unnoticed by the commuters. After a moment or two, I allowed myself to exhale. The train rolled on. The commuters generally sat quietly. We pulled into a stop at the next station. The recorded voice of the CTA sounded out over the PA congenially, "Wellington."

I took another breath. Scanning my eyes over the variety of faces on the train, I continued to go unnoticed. Thank God. I cracked the book open in my lap. Where to start? Flipping to the index at the back of the book, I looked down through the listings. I didn't even know what I should be looking for. Dragging my finger down to the word *evil*, I was shocked by the sheer number of page listings. Even the thought of checking each one was exhausting. I flipped to the first page.

The primary listing for *evil* was predictably vague and had the word *See...* followed by other terms to look up and trailed by more page numbers. It was like a choose-your-own-adventure story. The train hurtled along. People climbed on and off as we made our way closer to the Loop.

I flipped through the pages of the encyclopedia, scanning through words and information, hungry for anything which might leap out as familiar. The listing for *poltergeist* rang a few bells. The furniture moving around on its own. The dead plants. The bruises left by an invisible hand. But the events I'd experienced hadn't been confined to my apartment or even the hotel. The definitions and examples under *possession* seemed fitting as well. The vicious changes in behavior. The unnatural strength. But nothing in those listings mentioned anything about the demon or spirit or whatever jumping from person to person.

The entry on *hauntings* definitely seemed to describe the happenings at the SCC, and when taken into account with the information Shafer had given me, it all started to make a lot of sense. Still, the stories and descriptions didn't match up with what I'd gone through, and I wasn't aware of anyone else who worked at the Rosebriar Room experiencing half of what I had. I went back to the index. There had to be something. As I moved my finger down the list of words, one stood out. *Death, near-death experiences, return from—* Just below, there was a sub-entry for *suicide*.

I flipped to the corresponding page number. I'd never really thought about the definition of death. It always seemed pretty straightforward. You're alive; then you're not. I'd never even given much thought to the idea of the afterlife. Growing up Catholic, if I was ever curious, there was a Bible full of answers or the priest to ask.

The book in my hands became very heavy. My wrists ached dully, and as I sat there, I couldn't help but think about what Bryan had said. The way he described finding me in the bathtub. About what had happened in the ambulance. Had I really wanted to kill myself, or hadn't I? It didn't really matter. I had succeeded to a point. My heart had stopped regardless of my intentions. Bryan had told me as much. That night was blurry in my memory. Maybe because I had been trying so hard to not think about it.

In so many ways, Kenny and my relationship had been perfect. And in other ways, in ways I tried to ignore, it really wasn't. He had only recently come out. He struggled to understand where I was coming from so often. When I'd come home, exhausted and needing to vent about my days' worth of microaggressions at the Rosebriar Room, more often than not, he would brush aside my experiences. I was being oversensitive. My coworkers didn't mean it like that. Not everything is racism. In retrospect, I guess he resented the fact that he couldn't understand that facet of my life. He liked to say he got it. Sure, he was white, but he was gay too; he understood what it was like to be marginalized. Maybe he truly wanted to get it. Maybe he earnestly wanted us to be able to understand each other completely. But I'd come to learn, when it comes down to it, intentions don't really matter too much at all.

God. I loved him so much. And love had made me blind. We were both each other's first boyfriends. First relationships. Firsts of so many things. I had imagined our wedding. I'd picked out the songs in my head. And when he told me he had drunkenly fucked a coworker at his office party—some white guy who considered himself to be straight—the earth fell out from beneath my feet. The guy, Graham, wasn't gay, but there was something special about Kenny. They had to keep things quiet, but Kenny wanted to see where things would go with him. As for me, I understood, right? Kenny and Graham made sense together. They fit. Nothing was lost in translation.

In the office together, they'd be two straight buddies since Kenny had never found himself in a position where he'd been compelled to come out to his coworkers. Then, outside of the office, they'd fuck. They'd be lovers. They'd be whatever it was they were, and I wasn't. I was nothing. And I knew it. That knowledge burrowed deep inside me. The pain and rage and all the dark, black fucking bile of rejection clouded my vision. I could feel it like a frozen hand squeezing my heart tighter and tighter. Breathing was hard. Everything was hard. Everything seemed impossible. This went on for months as Kenny moved out of our home and then in with Graham. I struggled to stay afloat. I tried to drink it away. I tried to dance it off. I was trying desperately to be okay. I was far from it.

Then one night, I went out to a bar in Boystown with some friends. And in walked Kenny and Graham. The same bar. A friend of a friend of mine was a bartender there. Kenny knew that. He knew it was the bar I liked to frequent when pals wanted to go dancing. Kenny hated dancing. Hated coming to Boystown. The go-go dancers and the grinding and the booze were just so *gay*. I don't know if it was some sort of insecurity in him, or maybe the reflexive pushing away of what he didn't like about himself. About me. But that night, there he was. With Graham. And there I was, alone in all the ways that mattered. So utterly, fucking pathetically alone.

I climbed in an Uber back to our...back to *my* apartment. Tears coursing down my face. Rageful and forlorn. I stumbled up the stairs. I turned on the water in the tub before heading to the kitchen. The world was tilting beneath me. My vision was blurred with tears or alcohol or both. I grabbed a mostly full handle of cheap shitty vodka from the top of the fridge. I grabbed a steak knife from the sink. I shed clothes as I went. A shoe here. My pants there, my phone still in the pocket. By the time I made it back to the bathroom, the tub was just shy of overflowing. Clumsily, I turned off the water. Climbed into the tub. Vodka in one hand. Knife in the other. I sat there. I chugged the booze. I clutched the knife. I laughed. I remember laughing. I remember the way it echoed across the tile of the bathroom. What was so funny?

My head was swimming and the absurdity of it all just seemed so fucking overwhelming. Everything was so ridiculous. It was like I was looking at myself and seeing what I was doing, and all I could do was laugh at how stupid and pathetic I was. I don't remember the pain. Not really. I do remember the water getting warmer around my hands and forearms. It made me think of being a small child, peeing in a pool. That thought made me laugh again. *Fuck you, Kenny. Fuck you, Graham. I'll be dead, and you'll be fucking sorry. I'll be dead, and I'll become a fucking ghost, and I'll fucking haunt you just the same fucking way you haunt me, you fucking asshole.* It was a self-indulgent, melodramatic, petulant, ridiculous stream of thoughts that, even in the moment, some distant floating part of me was embarrassed and ashamed to have to claim as mine. And that's what I can remember. That's what I had been trying so hard to forget.

The recorded voice of the CTA rang out, "Merchandise Mart." I was downtown. The demographics of the train car had shifted slightly and were now even whiter and more male than it had been when I got on. Finance bros and office drones crowded the train with their iPhones in hand, *The New Yorker* in their laps. Brown leather messenger bags and briefcases were at every one of their sides, and all of them had their eyes firmly focused on me.

All at once, each of their pale faces broke into the same identical grin. The grin stretched their mouths, agonizing bit by bit, into a hungry crescent. Wide and humorless. The doors of the train slammed shut, and the momentum picked up as we raced toward the next stop. It would take maybe two minutes to make it to the Washington and Wells stop. Could I last that long, or would these men tear me to shreds by then? In my chest, my heart began to pound rapidly.

My eyes darted from face to face. All their eyes shared the same glassy look. Their pupils were dilated. Their expanded pupils made their irises seem almost entirely black. Shark eyes. I stood as carefully as possible. All the men that had been sitting did the same. I froze. It was as though any sudden movement might cause them to attack. Above me, the fluorescent lights of the train flickered and died. The train car was full of shadows. The thin gray light of the late afternoon—at least what could filter through the canyons of downtown skyscrapers—bounced off the aluminum interior of the train with gloomy cold light.

Quietly at first, a chorus of low growling laughter that seeped through gritted teeth started to fill the train car. The PA system dinged to life. A low guttural scream-hoarse voice spoke out from the speakers overhead: "You're mine." Inch by inch, I made my way toward the doors. All the men seemed almost frozen as I moved past them as quietly as I could. It was like winding my way through a sculpture garden full of living statues. I could hear their teeth grinding in their heads. Their grins so wide, jaws clenched with an impossible tension. They didn't sway with the movement of the train. They were rigid. Hard. As though each of them had rigor mortis. Unable to avoid it, I looked down at them. Straining against their pants, each and every one of these men had a raging erection. It was absurd and grotesque.

A manic giggle slipped from between my lips. I felt like I was losing my mind. I continued to slip through the crowd as delicately as I could, trying desperately to not make physical contact with the forest of frozen commuters. Only their jaws, grinding away, and their eyes, tracking my movements, moved at all. I was almost there.

Then, with a sudden lurch, the train turned a sharp corner as it entered the Loop, slowing as it made the curve. I lost my balance and tumbled into the nearest of the men. It was as though an electrical current had been keeping them paralyzed, and in an instant, the circuit was broken; the current cut off. They all started moving at once. Fast. A single entity with countless hands, and each of these hands was grabbing at me. Pulling me. Tearing at me. Overhead, the PA system dinged again, the voice's laugh echoing through the car. In my pocket, I could feel my phone vibrate as it rang.

Hard hands grabbed me everywhere. Fingers wriggling and stabbing into me as they dug into my flesh. My arms, my chest, my ass. Ripping at my clothes. Hands grabbed at my crotch hungrily. I could hear the horde's collective teeth gnashing grotesquely. All the bodies were on me at once, surrounding me, engulfing me utterly from everywhere. I could feel their bodies press against mine. I could feel the stabbing press of their hard cocks pushed against me. Fingers forced their way into my mouth down my throat. Hands were tearing at the seat of my pants as digging fingers tried to make their way inside me.

Desperately, I pushed against the bodies. Using the heavy thickness of the encyclopedia, I beat away the hands and bodies as well as I could. Inch by fucking inch, I fought my way toward the doors. I could barely breathe.

There were hands choking me, grabbing at my throat. I somehow managed to press my back against the sliding doors. Before me, the horde of fiendishly smiling men reached toward me. Below me, I could feel the momentum of the train start to slow.

We lurched to a sudden stop. Behind me, with a metallic *whoosh*, the doors slid open, and I fell out of the car, landing flat on my back on the platform. The confused commuters at Clark and Lake, waiting for the train, didn't seem to notice. They started to push their way onto the train. As fast as I could, I rolled to my feet and ran from the train car. I stumbled to the stairs, taking them two at a time until I made it to the street below.

Chapter Nineteen

Eyes closed, I leaned against the cold stone of a building. Above me, it stretched toward the sky. The sun had further set, and in the shadows of the Loop, I tried to stabilize myself. I hurt everywhere. My throat was raw. I realized I must have been screaming on the train. The fabric of my clothes had held for the most part, but there were tears and stretches. My heart still beat away rapidly in my chest. Passersby on the street kept their distance. I must have looked crazy, standing there with tears streaming down my face. I didn't care.

Shaky breaths went in and out from between my lips. I bent over, hands on my knees, and gently put my head between my legs, lowering into a crouched fetal position. I remember being told by someone that it was the best way to stave off a panic attack or hyperventilation or something. My head was a blur. I realized the book was nowhere to be found. I must have left it on the platform. Or the train.

Looking down at myself, I noticed countless welts and finger marks in my flesh. Red and angry. Gingerly, I looked at my wrists. The cotton had turned almost entirely a reddish pink. Remarkably, the bandages hadn't been torn off by the rough hands that had grabbed my wrists, pulling my hands toward bulging crotches. I shook off the thought. Shook off the memory.

Standing, I wiped the tears from my face with my pink-tinged shirt sleeves. I was at the corner of Wells and Madison. In my pocket, my phone vibrated briefly. On the screen a voice mail notification popped up. I recalled the voice mail from that morning. What more could that fucking voice have to say? Was it even worth listening to? It occurred to me that I shouldn't have deleted the first voice mail. It could have been proof I wasn't crazy. Having a recording of some evil disembodied entity's voice could only be useful in terms of proving what had been going on. But proving it to who?

I pulled my wallet out of my back pocket and dug out the business card I had stashed there that morning. If this voice mail was what I thought it must be, I'd have something substantial I could show to Detective Hendricks. That and the bruises covering my body had to be worth something. What sort of help the police might be able to offer, I had no clue. But it had to be worth the try. First, I'd need to listen to the voice mail.

Hesitantly, I tapped the notification. A single word sounded in my ear. "Come." It was a simple command. Almost a whisper. I knew what it meant. I thought back to the story from the ghost tour. That one tourist had to return to Hull House to return whatever spirit had latched onto them. I would have to do the same. If I ever wanted to bring an end to all this, I had to return to the Sentinel Club. I had to go back to the Rosebriar Room.

I started to walk toward the hotel. It was on the opposite side of the Loop from where I stood. Taking the train was out of the question. I honestly didn't know if I'd be able to take the goddamn CTA ever again, but that was a concern that would have to wait. At that moment, there were maybe six blocks between me and my destination.

The walk would take maybe fifteen minutes. I was in no rush. I took a deep breath and started to walk.

I looked down at the business card in my hand. After a moment, I dialed the phone number. "You've reached Detective Hendricks. I'm unavailable to answer the phone right now, but leave your name, number, and a detailed message, and I'll return your call as soon as I can. If this is an emergency, please dial 911." Her calm voice eased any doubts I had.

"Hi, yes, this is Gabe Espinosa...from this morning. You told me to call and...um, this is hard to explain, but weird things have been happening since the...the attack, uh...since. All day, weird guys have been, I dunno, threatening me...and I've been getting weird calls and then on the train...I was... I uh—I was assaulted on the train and... I dunno." I pulled the phone away from my face so she wouldn't hear me choke for air. I rushed to wipe my eyes and then took a deep breath before beginning again. "I don't know. I just wanted to call you. Uh. I got a weird voice mail saying to go back to the Rosebriar...and I'm going. Maybe I'm crazy to go, but I'm going, so...I wanted to...I don't know...I just thought you should know." I hung up. "I'm such an idiot." I stuffed my phone in my pocket. "Fuck."

Calling Detective Hendricks might have been a mistake. She'd only have questions. Questions that I didn't have any answers to. Questions better left unasked, especially for a guy with a fairly recent stay in a mental ward. If things went as hoped at the Rosebriar, if returning really would bring an end to all this, then maybe it wouldn't matter. But if it didn't go as I hoped? If the end brought about by me returning to the SCC was one, I'd rather not think too much about...then maybe it was a good thing that I called her. I wish I knew.

The Sentinel Club towered over me as I approached. The sidewalk outside of the main entrance had been cleared of any glass and splinters from that morning, though yellow police tape still circled the crater of smashed concrete where the table had crashed. I walked into the lobby. The employee entrance was around the back. In the alley. But in order to get into the hotel proper and the Rosebriar on the thirteenth floor, I'd have to go through the basement complex. Whatever nerve I had that gave me the guts to come back here had its limits. I would not set foot in that subterranean maze. The shining chandelier that hung from the lobby's high ceiling was reflected in the polished marble of its floor. Guests milled around while a couple of bell boys pushed carts of luggage down the hall. Beyond the reception desk, the twin gazes of the Adonis statues looked down on me from their posts at the top of the marble stairs.

I don't know what I was expecting. It's not like they would shut down the hotel. I hadn't expected them to turn out the guests unlucky enough to be staying there. But I was surprised at just how normal things were. It was like nothing had happened at all. I couldn't help but marvel at it as I tried to work up the nerve to walk further into the hotel. Only a couple of hours ago, a table had plummeted thirteen floors, splintering and shattering into the still-cracked pavement. Only a few feet from that, a woman currently hand-fed a Pomeranian she was carrying in an oversized purse, completely oblivious.

I went to the concierge desk. "Hey, Stanley."

"Good afternoon, sir. How can I help you?" he said without looking up. As he finished what he was doing, he glanced my way. "Oh, Gabe, Hey, man. Sorry. Lot of incident reports and stuff to get through. How are you? What are you doing here?"

"I've got some stuff to take care of. What's up with the Rosebriar? I went home...after but hadn't really heard from anyone."

Stanley looked up at me, a bit embarrassed. "You'd think you guys would be closed for the day, but nope. From what I understand, y'all reopen for dinner service a little later than usual but..." He consulted a memo on the Rosebriar Room's embossed stationery. "By six thirty, y'all will be open for business."

"Classy."

"The classiest." He looked around the lobby. "It's like people around here are only worried about making money and avoiding inconvenience."

Stanley's sarcasm would typically prompt a laugh. As it was, I managed a small smile. "Yeah."

"How are you?" He looked at me, concerned. "No offense, man, but you look like shit. You okay?"

"Not really, but thanks."

"Shouldn't you be, I dunno, not here? If that shit went down with me, I'd never set foot in this place again." I looked at my phone. Five thirty. I'd have thirty minutes before pre-shift would start and an hour until the restaurant would open. Whatever I was supposed to do, or was supposed to happen, had better get to it.

"Yeah, I just...have to take care of something here."

"Two weeks' notice?"

"You know what? Yeah." This time, I couldn't help but laugh. Looking at Stanley, I realized how much I appreciated working with him, especially in a place like this. In his bright brown eyes, I could see a glaze of concern. I shot him a quick wave and headed for the rear service elevator. With one last glance around the beautiful hotel lobby, I headed for the Rosebriar Room.

The elevator doors slammed shut behind me and I was immediately claustrophobic. I jammed my finger into the thirteen button on the elevator's panel. I had no clue what to expect. I was flying blind here. There were no instructions for this. All I had to go on was an anecdote from a tour guide and a stupid fucking cryptic-ass voice mail telling me to come. Well, I had. Now what?

As the elevator crawled its way up the thirteen floors to the restaurant, I could feel my stomach twisting itself into knots. This was a bad idea. A very bad idea. The numbers in the panel indicating the elevator's current floor ticked past ten. Then eleven. Just as it was rolling onto twelve, the elevator came to a shuddering stop.

"No...no, no, no. You've got to be fucking kidding me."

I jammed my finger into the Door Open button repeatedly. The lights above me flickered. A groaning of metal filled the space. It had to be the elevator gears turning. Twisting. Pulling me up to the thirteenth floor. But what if it was something else? It sounded almost like a groaning voice.

"Fuck this." I shoved my fingers into the seam between the sliding doors. With all the strength in my fingers and hands, I pried the doors open.

The elevator was halfway between the floors. Most of the elevator was still stuck on eleven, but from the height of my shoulders up, the elevator opened to the twelfth. My face was just at the level of the floor. Before my eyes I could see the shining polished hardwood floor stretching out in front of me.

"Hello? Can someone help please? Please. The elevator is stuck."

There was no answer, but the warm light of the vintage incandescent light bulbs cast long shadows that shortened as they neared the elevator. The twelfth floor was where the suites were.

From somewhere down the hall I could hear music. It sounded like swing or jazz. Something instrumental, upbeat. It echoed down the hallway, making so that I couldn't be sure where exactly it was coming from; if the source of the music was near or far. But then, the sounds of footsteps and muffled voices became increasingly clear.

"Hey? Can someone help me, please?"

From just outside of my field of vision, I could hear the voices gain intensity. The people seemed to be arguing.

"Sir, I said no!" A pair of shiny black leather shoes filled the gap through which I could see part of the hall. They were joined by a pair of fancy wingtips, the sort I had never seen outside of an old movie or a black-and-white photo.

The shiny shoes moved to walk away from the wingtips, and then there was the cracking sound that reminded me of a bat striking a baseball. With a cry of pain, the man in the black shoes fell to the ground hard, followed by a billiards cue joining him on the floor with a clatter. I realized the sound I'd heard was this man being struck in the skull.

He had to be around my age. Maybe younger. Blood matted his hair and had started to drip on the polished hardwood floor as he writhed in pain. I could only see flashes of the scene through the space between the elevator doors, but he seemed to be wearing an old service uniform. It was the kind that the SCC had required its porters to wear way back in the day. The same kind of uniform they made us put on for Halloween as a part of the Roaring Twenties–themed celebrations the hotel would throw. The porter groaned. He moved groggily, and the man in wingtips stood over him.

"What the fuck? Hey!" I cried from the elevator. I tried to reach my arm out through the door, but with the height of the elevator, I could barely get my forearm into the hallway. "What the hell are you doing?"

The men in the hall seemed unable to hear me. I tried to shove the doors wider apart, but they wouldn't budge. Then, the man in wingtips was on top of the porter. From what I could tell, he was wearing a tuxedo. I could hear the rustling of fabric tearing, clasps being undone, and from my vantage point, I caught glimpses of pants getting torn down. I could hear the porter's muffled groans of refusal.

"Stop it! Hey, get off of him!" My cries fell on deaf ears. I couldn't do anything. I could see the bodies writhing on top of each other in a heap. The voice of the porter yelled out in pain and desperation, but the sound of the jazz music from down the hall seemed to drone louder and louder. Then the tuxedoed man grunted rhythmically as he thrust into the porter.

"Shut your spic mouth," the man in the tuxedo ordered between heavy breaths.

I jammed my finger into the button marked twelve on the elevator's panel. I slammed my fist against the Door Open button. The Emergency Call button. Any button that might get the elevator to do something. Anything. In my limited frame of vision, I could make out the pale flesh of a white hand pinning the porter's brown wrist against the polished wood floor. The sound of moaning and grunting and the slap of flesh against flesh was drowned out by the jazz music that flooded from down the hall.

"Stop it! Fucking stop it! *Stop!*" I screamed to no avail.

The elevator doors slammed shut, grazing the skin of my nose. With a lurch, the elevator started to ascend again, and with a ding, it came to an abrupt stop. The elevator fully arrived on the twelfth floor, and I braced myself to leap out the door. To push the tuxedoed man off the porter. To do whatever I might have to. The elevator doors slid open. There was nothing there. No porter. No tuxedoed man. No music. Nothing but an empty hallway, illuminated by the vintage light bulbs the designers had specifically chosen during the hotel's restoration process.

At my sides, my hands trembled. They were clenched into fists so tightly that my fingers ached. I flexed my fingers loose, and my knuckles cracked loudly in the now-quiet hallway. I stepped back onto the elevator. The button for the thirteenth floor was still illuminated, expectantly. I pressed the door close button and continued my ascent.

Chapter Twenty

I stepped out of the service elevator into the kitchen only to find the place in the middle of prepping for dinner service. From across the room of white tile and chrome, Rod was instructing the line cooks. I tried to shake off what I had seen on the twelfth floor. I was almost dizzy. Blood and adrenaline were pumping through my veins. I could feel heat in my face.

Beyond the stove ranges and flashing knives, Rod directed the kitchen staff about their prep work. He was focused, brow furrowed in concentration. Every now and then, he'd bark some command or snarl some criticism at the folks buzzing about the busy kitchen. Absurdly, the recollection of Rod's hand on the nape of my neck flew into my mind, and out of nowhere, I found myself ashamed and confused. Being in this place was seriously fucking with me. As if he could feel my gaze, Rod looked up. I spun and headed for the dining room, hoping he'd be too busy to follow.

Compared to the frantic bustle of the kitchen, the actual Rosebriar Room was quiet, still. The front-of-house staff wouldn't be here for pre-shift for another twenty minutes at least. A thick velvet curtain tastefully covered the portion of the window that had been smashed through that morning. Hidden behind the velvet, coarse plywood had been used to board up the gaping hole of the shattered Tiffany glass. The sun, now in the western part of the sky, offered only a burnt-orange sunset, fading into the horizon of Lake Michigan. Streaks of red clouds reflected off the crystal glasses spread across the dining room's place settings; all of which shone like rubies in the shadowy restaurant. Rubies. Or blood.

What might, at any other time or place, be a relaxing view of the lake at sunset here only served to set my nerves on edge. I was being watched. I had the distinct sensation eyes of unseen patrons from across the decades were gazing hungrily at me from the shadows. Whispers hung like cobwebs in the booths, and despite my being alone in this part of the restaurant, I knew I wasn't the only one there.

I looked around, expectant. I had followed the voice mail's directions. I was here. I had listened to the tour guide's story. I'd returned to this place. Now what? If I walked out of here and never looked back, would I be free to go? Would this be the end of it? Should I brush off my shoulders, give my limbs a quick shake out, and call it a day? I could only hope that returning here might be enough to leave behind whatever it was that had been fluttering around me like an angry moth since this morning.

At a loss, I muttered to the empty room, "So...is that it?"

From behind me, a hand wrapped around my arm, pressing gently into one of my countless new bruises. I cried out in pain and surprise, pulling away from a startled Rod.

"Woah! Sorry, hey, hey. Sorry! Gabe. It's me"

"Rod. Goddammit! What the fuck?" I made a wide circle, trying to catch my breath as I walked.

"Sorry! I'm sorry." Rod looked at me as though I were a horse caught in a storm. One more clap of thunder and I could bolt. Or trample him. A long moment passed. "You look like shit."

That was the second time I'd heard that in the past hour. It was an accurate appraisal. Taking a quick look down at myself, I realized I was still wearing most of what I had worn to work that morning. Only now, my cheap H&M suit was wrinkled and tattered. The white sleeves of my shirt had turned a deep pink at the wrists. I could only imagine what my face must look like. I'm sure the manic glaze in my eyes could only bring the whole look together. Manic-chic. No wonder Stanley had been concerned.

"Are you okay?"

"Not particularly. No."

I resented the fact that, as raggedy as I must have looked, he looked good. I didn't want to notice the impeccable white linen of his chef's frock. He had his bandana folded into a neat band at his forehead, keeping his brown hair back and out of his striking blue eyes. I had a lot of other, far more pressing things to think about than his perfectly groomed stubble and the tattoos crawling up his arms. Once more, I was filled with shame for indulging in the distraction of Chef Rod's looks. But why should I feel ashamed? Over the course of my employment here, I'd seen how Rod had maneuvered through his interactions with the female staff. I'd witnessed how he'd carefully curate his appearance; how he'd take advantage of his looks and reputation to his own ends.

As quick as the shame had risen in me, it turned to anger. "You almost gave me a fucking heart attack!"

"Sorry! Look, I saw you in the kitchen, I just wanted to talk real fast. What are you doing here?"

I averted my eyes. "I came to—I'm actually...I'm here to give my notice. I'm done. Just had to stop by and...I don't think I'm coming back." I don't think I had realized the truth of the statement until the words came out of my mouth. But it was true. All the horrors of the day aside, I didn't want to work here anymore. My life had been a mess for long enough. Something needed to change.

"Is this about this morning?"

"You mean when I was randomly attacked in this very fucking room? Yeah, might have something to do with it." I thought about what I'd seen on the twelfth floor. I thought about the train. I thought about what Shafer had told me about this place. "I need to be done with all of this."

"Right. But, I mean, it's not about the kiss."

Exhaustingly, a stubborn, familiar flash of heat bloomed in my neck. Was I really so desperate for affection that at any sign of interest, of potential intimacy, could distract me so easily? All it took was Rod merely mentioning our kiss, and I was lost, remembering his lips on mine, and the feel of his stupid fucking stubble against my cheek. That something so insignificant could unmoor me so utterly could only mean one thing. I had to be the most pathetic man alive.

"Listen. I just wanted to apologize. I don't know what came over me. I mean, don't take this the wrong way, but...I'm straight."

"Right. No, yeah. I knew that."

"So...I don't really know what...that was."

"Don't worry about it."

He looked at me abashed. His embarrassment at the thought of kissing me was humiliating. Then, in an instant, something changed. It was like a light switch flipped. One second, Rod was a good five feet away, and the next there was no space between us. Our mouths made contact with such force, I could hear our teeth clack. His tongue found its way into my mouth as his hands found their way everywhere else. Without me realizing it, we were on the floor, limbs entangled, right in the center of the empty dining room.

Almost every part of me was tender and bruised, but all I could do was wince and adjust. There was no fighting it. Part of me knew I shouldn't want whatever this was. Warning bells were going off somewhere in my mind. But this wasn't like before. This wasn't like the others. I knew Rod. He wasn't some intercontinental hotel guest. This wasn't some random jogger or strangers on the train. I had known him and wanted him, whether I wanted to admit it to myself or not. He was desired by half the staff. And in this moment, he wanted me. Better to leave the *why* of that desire unquestioned. Yet, part of me knew better. Part of me was still afraid. Then, like always, my mind fluttered to Kenny. Kenny didn't want me anymore. But right now, Rod did. The rest was silence.

Rod's fingers intertwined with mine, pinning my hands above my head. Straddling my waist, his legs locked mine to the ground. With a toss of his head, he flung the length of his brown hair back over his shoulder and pulled his face from mine. Our eyes locked. He drove his pelvis against mine, and I could fill his stiffness straining against the thick linen of his pants.

Then, his face, which seconds ago had been a cloud of confused lust, shifted again. In an instant, a mask of gleeful hate burned through that cloud, cracking his mouth into an ever-widening grin. His eyes were fixed points of madness, glaring into mine. I couldn't move. I had let myself be pinned to the floor. I struggled in his grasp but couldn't shift out from beneath his weight. He might as well have been made of stone.

Above me I could see his jaw muscles tightening and tightening, and I could hear the sickening crunch of his teeth grinding against one another. His rough calloused hands slid down my wrists and up my arms, painful and heavy. They found their way to my throat as I struggled to pound my fists against his chest, his shoulders, and his face—anywhere my blows could land. It was like striking a boulder. He didn't flinch or wince or react at all except for tightening his grip around my throat.

I couldn't scream. I couldn't think. Frantically, I slapped my hands against the immovable mass of his torso. I reached for his face, desperately reaching my fingers for the vulnerability of his eyes, but he stretched his neck, veins bulging with the effort, wrenching his face from my grasp. I couldn't breathe. Against my will, my eyes started to roll back in my head. My vision swam, and I drunkenly took in the room. In the shadows of the Rosebriar, pale faces stared out at me from the shadows. So many eyes watching us. So many smiles grinning in my failing vision.

After a moment, all I could feel was a well of sorrow and desperation give way to an abyss of hopelessness. All I could do was close my eyes and wait for the inevitable. Somewhere in the darkness beyond my eyelids, I could hear him laugh. A low, broken, keening sound. In a voice that sounded like many at once, coming together in a chorus that was deep and growling, he said, "This is where it began. And this is where it will end."

Out of nowhere, a sudden sharp crack sounded, echoed by a loud metallic clang, and Rod's stranglehold lifted. I gasped in a choked, painful breath. Air flooded my desperate lungs. Coughing, I forced my eyes open as Chef Rod tumbled off me with the force of the unseen blow. I dragged myself away from the mass of his crumpled body. In a daze, I made it to my knees, heaving and shaky.

Standing over us, eyes fixed firmly on Rod, was Leslie. Unlike me, she had changed out of her work uniform since I'd seen her talking to the police that morning. Her slight frame rose and fell as she heaved with the effort of her labored breathing. Clutched in her white-knuckled hands was the heavy metal flower vase from the bar. The massive bronze satyr grinned there, still raised above her shoulder where the follow-through of her swing landed it. Flowers and scented water were scattered around us, and Leslie's face was frozen in a mixture of panic and exhilaration.

"This is so fucked up. What the fuck?!" Dropping the vase with a clang, she brought her shaking hands to her mouth. "What did I just do?" Flat on his back, Rod's chest rose and fell, shallowly, barely visible. "Is he dead?"

"I don't think so." My voice came out quiet and breathy.

"Are...are you okay?" She sank to the floor herself, eyes watering. I couldn't find the words to answer her. My arms had grown heavy, but gradually I managed to crawl over to her, and I pulled her into a hug. It was something I would never have imagined happening prior to that moment, but there it was.

"Thank you." I managed to whisper. In my arms, Leslie proceeded to melt into a trembling, sobbing mess. She allowed herself to stay in my arms for a moment more, then climbed to her feet. Pulling her phone out of her pocket, she looked down at Rod before stabbing her manicured finger at her phone's screen three times.

"I quit! I fucking quit! I don't want to work in this creepy-ass place anymore. I quit! Oh my God." She held her phone to her face. From where I sat, I could hear the phone ringing and then the muffled voice of the 911 operator.

"Me too, Leslie," I muttered to myself. "Me too."

Beyond the Tiffany-glass windows, the sky had settled into a deep purple, the color of a bruise. The sun had set. Leslie paced back and forth, already relating what had just happened to the operator.

Overhead the chandelier cast light down on the Rosebriar Room. It glinted on the silver anchor still wrapped around my wrist. Gingerly, I unfastened the bracelet Kenny had given me. Rod gave a small groan. Between us, the bronze satyr vase grinned threateningly. Still erect. Still obscene. Slowly, I stood and tossed the bracelet into the now empty vase.

"I'll be downstairs." I said, not really worried if Leslie had heard me or not. If the police wanted to take my statement, they could do it in the lobby.

Chapter Twenty-One

I set down my empty coffee cup and looked around. The patio of the cafe was relatively empty. The sun was hot overhead, but a spring breeze kept the afternoon cool. In the months since I stopped working at the Rosebriar Room, I'd cut down my coffee intake by nearly 70 percent. I no longer had to wake up at such an ungodly hour and no longer needed to gulp down my hot coffee as fast as I could while tucked away in the barista station, avoiding my manager. Nevertheless, I still tended to down a cup of coffee faster than I usually meant to. Old habits die hard.

In my pocket, my cell phone began to vibrate. I'd been expecting the call. "Hi, Detective Hendricks. How are you?"

"Doing well. And you, Mr. Espinosa?"

"Honestly, not too bad." Since November, Detective Hendricks and I had gotten to know each other relatively well. When Leslie called the police that night, Detective Hendricks was the first person on the scene. She was already on her way to the Sentinel Club to follow up the voice mail I had left her. "Any news?"

"Yes, actually. The judge has officially set the date for the trial. It'll be next week." I took a breath. I was going to need more coffee. This whole ordeal was exhausting. "Thursday."

"Thursday?"

"Yes, May 10th. Are you writing this down?" I wasn't.

"Well, do I have to be there?"

"Have to? No. The district attorney has your testimony on record, but—" I had grown to appreciate Detective Hendricks's straightforwardness. "—I think it would be good for you to be there." She wasn't harsh necessarily, but always spoke her mind. "For the others."

I considered it for a moment before responding. "All right. I can make that work." She was right. I should be at Rod's trial. But that didn't make it something I was looking forward to. "Was there anything else?"

"Nope. You taking care of yourself?"

"I'm doing my best." I was.

"That's what I like to hear. We'll talk soon."

"Okay. Laters."

I looked down at my phone's screen. After a moment, I opened up a blank text message and typed *Trial, May 10th*, and then I sent it to myself. With a ding, the message popped back up in my inbox. I wouldn't forget the date.

Rod was obviously not in his right mind when he attacked me. I knew that. He probably wasn't in his right mind when he kissed me either. I knew he was under the influence of whatever darkness had been accumulating in the Sentinel Club over the years. However, Rod apparently had been in his right mind on the night he assaulted Sofia, the line cook from the Rosebriar. He'd also been in his right mind the morning he assaulted Cecilia in dry storage. Rod had been under no influence but his own on the multiple occasions he had assaulted various other female members of the kitchen staff who had cycled through the restaurant during his time there. The fact that no one reported the incidents was unsurprising. I'm sure there were even more women he preyed on that never would report what happened, but a number of them had. After the incident with me, as documented by the security cameras and witnessed by Leslie, Sofia, Cecilia, and the others came around to the idea that someone might actually listen. Someone might actually believe them.

It was a hard thing to be happy about. When I looked back on everything that happened, I struggled with the idea that I should be glad I went through what I did at the SCC. Yet, at the same time, regretting it wouldn't change anything. Wishing it hadn't happened to me wouldn't change things. Why wish it had happened to someone else when it already had?

Ultimately, something good did come out of it all. Even still, going through the entire fucking judicial system was a nightmare unto itself. Everything was a pain in the ass. Not to mention the fact that it was impossible to explain the less rational details of what had happened without lying. Or at least without sounding like a crazy person. And that was something I was not.

I never doubted my sanity for a second. I know what I saw. I know what I heard. I know what I felt, and honestly, I was still haunted by it. I don't know if I'll ever be entirely free from the marks it all left me with. That didn't mean I had to waste my breath trying to convince Detective Hendricks, who I'd found to be a no-nonsense rationalist, to believe in the supernatural. I didn't need to.

The stranger from that morning went back to Stockholm after being released from the hospital. The doctors deemed the incident to be some sort of epileptic fit, and that was that. As far as Rod was concerned, his own criminal behavior more or less explained what he did while under the thrall of the entity, or energy, or whatever. That was enough for Detective Hendricks and any other curious parties.

As Detective Hendricks had told me, "The simplest explanation usually turns out to be the truth." But I'd come to learn that truth is relative and often stranger than we'd like to accept. I knew the truth of my experience at the Sentinel Club. So did Maisey and Bryan. That was enough. And since I made my final return to the Rosebriar Room, nothing supernatural or anything of the like had happened to me. That was more than enough to be thankful for.

"Sorry I'm late!" With the scraped groan of metal chair against brick patio, Stephen pulled out the seat across from me and sat down. "Did you finish your coffee already?"

"I was just about to order another one actually." I couldn't help but smile.

"Let me! To make up for being late. Besides I'm gonna need some caffeine myself!" Jumping up from the seat he'd just plopped into, Stephen headed into the cafe. Almost immediately, he bounded back out and gave me a peck on the lips. "Hi, by the way."

"Hi." This time he actually did make it into the cafe, leaving me to my smiling.

In mid-December or so, I got a notice from the Chicago Public Library that the copy of *The Encyclopedia of the Paranormal,* which I had checked out, was officially overdue. When I went into the Merlo Branch to explain that I'd lost it on the train, Stephen just so happened to be working the desk. We made small talk, and he slyly removed my lost book fees from the system. Apparently, he'd gone through a bit of a breakup and was feeling generous. One thing led to another and we'd been officially dating since January.

From time to time, I would still think of Kenny. The scars on my wrists would never disappear completely, though they had healed over. I'd still have nightmares about the Rosebriar. I'd still find myself being sad or angry or both about everything that I went through. But sitting on the patio of that cafe in that moment, with the sun shining on my face, I could look at the scars on my wrists and see them for what they were. Not a sign of weakness. Not proof of how pathetic I was capable of being, how pathetic I could consider myself to be. Those scars were a testament to what I had been able to survive. After all, scars only appear after a wound heals.

At least, that's how I could look at them for that moment. In the sunshine. With a kiss fresh on my lips. A smile on my face. The moment would pass, as all moments do. I was just as likely to wake up one morning and be unable to see anything in my scars other than ugly reminders of one of my biggest mistakes. But ultimately, those moments would pass too.

About the Author

Jose Nateras is a writer, actor, and improviser/comedian from Chicago. Holding his MFA in writing from the School of the Art Institute of Chicago (SAIC), he also has a BA in theatre from Loyola University Chicago, where he minored in international film and media studies. Over the course of his decade-plus career as an actor on stage and screen, Jose has also been working as a writer, poet, and storyteller. From writing as a freelance journalist for various publications—covering topics such as arts news, book reviews, and media criticism—to writing his debut novel, *Testament*, Jose has stretched himself as an artist, writing numerous full-length stage plays and screenplays, as well as shorts. As a student, his short play *The Interview* won him Best Playwright in L.U.C.'s Loyola Dionysia and his short film *Cell Phone Time Machine* won First Place in the L.U.C. IFMS/Ignition Sci-Fi Movie Contest. In 2019, he was honored as one of Windy City Times 30 Under 30 for making "substantial contributions to the Chicagoland LGBT Community in the fields of entertainment, politics, health, activism, academics, sports, or other areas." Jose spends his free time watching tons of TV and movies, at comedy shows, at the theatre, reading, social media-ing, and staying physically active.

Email: josenateras@gmail.com

Facebook: www.facebook.com/Jose.Nateras.39

Twitter: @JoseNateras

Website: www.josenateras@gmail.com

Also Available from NineStar Press

Connect with NineStar Press

www.ninestarpress.com

www.facebook.com/ninestarpress

www.facebook.com/groups/NineStarNiche

www.twitter.com/ninestarpress

www.tumblr.com/blog/ninestarpress